HOUR OF SECRETS

UNHOLY ANGLES
BOOK 2

KAT LE VEQUE

OLIVERHEBERBOOKS

AUTHOR'S NOTE

They're known as The Unholy Angels.

What a great group of guys this is. I had such a great time writing about them and, in a couple of cases, expanding the stories. Originally, these were separate stories published under different titles, but I really wanted to make this a cohesive group. The guys are all the same age and literally have the same backgrounds, so The Unholy Angels was born—a CIA unit so elite that it's considered the best in the world. The guys in this series, so far—Trace, Reed, and Beau—are considered the best of the best. Hard-core, hard-hitting agents who fight for what they believe in. But then, the twist—these are hard-core agents who eventually retire and try to settle back down into civilian life.

That's a tough one.

It's like driving a car 100 MPH for years and then suddenly hitting the brakes and being expected to be okay with that. Being expected to blend in with the normal world around them and assume a normal life. That's the tough part, but the guys do it well and, of course, falling in love is a major part of that.

These stories, however, deal with heavy subjects—assault, murder, racial injustice, and betrayal to name a few. But at the core of the stories is a message: hope. There is always hope. Hope for love, hope for healing, and any number of other 'hopes.' This is a series that introduces a lot of subjects and, hopefully, does it with strength and tact. The bottom line is that these are great guys and I love watching them handle life as it comes at them and eventually fall in love. For good.

Each story in the series starts out with a mission that shows a pivotal moment in the lives of the agents. It explains the stuff they'd dealt with and gives a little background on how they fought—and survived—their job. The heroes definitely have a connection and that continues into their civilian life.

The books in this series can be read in any order:

Hour of Surrender
Hour of Dreams
Hour of Secrets

Just three for now, but there will be more at some point. Until then -

Happy reading!

THE UNHOLY ANGELS

In the Hebrew Bible, a 'destroying angel' is an entity sent by God to dispense His wrath. In the old and new testament, nothing is feared more than the angel of death. In this day and age, nothing is feared more than the specialized CIA unit known as The Unholy Angels.

They come from all walks of life, both military and non-military families. But each man has a military background and training, and each man has decided to go above and beyond for his fellow man. They have become agents, operatives with names like the General, the Intimidator, the Fixer, and more. In the name of justice and freedom, they live by the sword and sometimes die by the sword. It's a world of constant pressure, constant danger, and when an agent transfers out or retires, they often find the real world difficult to live in.

They must find their way.

Meet the men of The Unholy Angels and the
women who love them.
Loyalty above all.
And a love that outshines the darkness.

IN THE BEGINNING
EARLY 2000S, MERSIN, TURKIYE

It had been a running gun battle.

They had what they'd come for, but now, in the heat of the late afternoon, those they'd been trying to evade had caught up to them. It didn't matter that they'd changed cars twice to throw them off the scent. That hadn't mattered at all. Through the dirty, dusty streets, avoiding pedestrians and power poles, they'd been fleeing the *Turk Mafyasi*.

The Turkish Mafia.

This was a lesser branch based in Adana, but they had contacts and family members all over the place. Trace, Marcos, Beau, and Reed had found that out the hard way. The op had been simple – extricating a mafia member who had killed a CIA agent and bring him to the ports at Mersin for transfer to a vessel that would take him to a U.S. Navy warship patrolling in the Mediterranean. They'd traced the killer of their friend to his sister's house in Adana and they'd burned down the house and killed about twelve people to get at him.

Now that they had him, they wanted to keep him.

No matter what the *Obalar Mafyasi* had to say about it.

The Obalar family was big in Adana. There had to be a thousand of them, all spread out over the city. A ruthless group that made their money in drugs and weapons and the agent they'd killed had been an undercover operative. A friend of the group of CIA men who were trying to bring his killer to justice.

They were known as The Unholy Angels.

And they were.

Destroyer angels.

"Beau!" Trace Rocklin shouted above the wind that was roaring in through the windows of the Fiat they were in. "You need to either go faster or try to lose these bastards. And watch the flank – they're trying to cut us off!"

Beau Meade, a man born and bred in Mississippi, had a cool way about him. He didn't get worked up about much. But that didn't mean he wasn't on top of what was going on around them.

He knew the stakes.

As soon as Trace shouted at him, he caught sight of a car shooting out at them from an alley up ahead. The car meant to cut them off, but Beau jerked the steering wheel to the left and managed to avoid them enough so that Trace could shoot out their windshield. That sent the car careening into one of the cars that was chasing them and they both went up in flames.

Beau took a hard left and disappeared down another street.

"Are agents meeting us at the port?" he yelled over the wind.

Before anyone could answer him, he had to duck low to dodge a volley of bullets that had just ripped over his head and pinged into the car frame. Trace and the two other men of their group lay down return fire, enough to rupture the tires of the pursuing car that was closest to them.

Beau took another hard right that nearly pitched Trace onto the street.

"There should be a line of Navy personnel at the port waiting for us," Trace said, gripping the car frame to keep his balance. "Reed? That's your department. We'll have reinforcements – right?"

Reed McCoy, who had come to the CIA after working for the NCIS division, slid into the back seat so he could reload his gun. He was still a Marine to the bone in spite of the fact he hadn't officially been one for years.

"Yeah," he said. On the floorboards below his feet, their prisoner was trying to push himself up and Reed put an enormous cowboy-booted foot on the back of the man's neck to shove him down again. "There should be some Marines ready to reinforce us when we get there."

Trace eyed the big man from Wyoming. "There had better be," he said. "Because we've got Obalar members coming out of our asses. If the Marines aren't there, we're dead."

"They'll be there."

More bullets zinged over their heads. Trace and Reed ducked, but Marcos, who was still returning fire, got winged on the jaw. He threw himself into the back seat, hand over the wound.

"Is it bad?" he asked Trace. "Look at it. Is it bad?"

Marcos was an excellent agent, but he could be excitable. Sissy was more like it. Trace shoved him forward, over the supine prisoner and into the passenger seat next to Beau.

"You'll live," he told him. "Help Beau. If anyone comes around aiming for him, take them out."

Marcos wasn't quite so sure that his good looks weren't forever damaged by the bullet graze, but he didn't say anything. Trace was too hard for his own good sometimes and especially in a crisis, but that's why he was one of the best in the business. The harder the job, the better he performed. The Russians even had a name for him - *istreblyat*.

The Eliminator.

It wasn't as if the others in the Unholy Angels weren't well known to their adversaries, either. There were others in their group, but these men were the core. They had been conducting deep ops for the CIA for about six years as a team and there wasn't one faction, group, or military leader who didn't know their names. Names, in addition to the Eliminator, like *covboy* – or Cowboy as Reed was known.

His adversaries were fascinated by the Marine from Wyoming who was like a real American hero. Beau, on the other hand, was called *komandir* - basically, the Commander or the General. Beau was the brains in situations like this, Trace was the hit man, and Reed was the muscle. Marcos was their communications guru. Adversaries didn't care much about him, but they should have – he was the one who kept the team moving.

Like now.

"There!" Marcos said, pointing off to the left. "The port. See it?"

Beau did. There were cars and shipping containers and buildings between them and the port of Mersin, but he wasn't going to let that get in his way. He drove over a curb, through a pathway, and emerged into the avenue along the beach on the other side. There were people in the way and Marcos hung his head out of the window, screaming for them to get out of the way. They scattered and Beau drove straight through, startling pigeons and seagulls and bottoming out on the curb.

Sparks flew from the under carriage.

More bullets flew overhead, but less than before. Their pursuers had either been lost or otherwise compromised. Or it could have been the fact that there was a dozen or so armed U.S. Marines on the dock, waiting by a small transport vessel to take them to the larger warship out at sea.

"There!" Trace shouted when he saw them. "Go, go, go!"

Beau headed straight for the Marines, who were ready

with their weapons. A few more bullets flew and the Marines returned fire as the Fiat flew off the road, jumped a curb, and hit part of a fence. The fence collapsed, partially on the car, but that didn't stop the men from bailing out of the vehicle and bringing their prisoner with them.

Safety was in sight.

Trace and Reed had the man by the arms, running for the dock and dragging his bound legs along the concrete. There were thousands of shipping containers around them because Mersin was a major port along the Mediterranean. In addition to the cargo ships, there were also several docked ships from the Turkish Navy. In all, it was an exceedingly crowded port and Reed and Trace managed to make it behind the line of Marines, who were covering their retreat along with Beau. He had a wicked-looking Colt M1A4 carbine rifle in his hands and as Reed and Trace ran past him, Beau followed, running backwards to cover them.

"Go, go!" Beau hissed, recognizing one of the cars that had been chasing them as it came around a corner of stacked cargo. "Hurry! Get in the boat!"

Marcos was already in the small landing craft that was docked at the end of a long pier. The pier had other ships lined up against it, so any bullets coming from their pursuers got lost in the steel and iron of the vessels. They had to run at least a quarter of a mile to get from the car to the landing craft, followed by the Marines at this point, and everyone bailed onto the vessel that took off the very second the last man was on board.

Out to sea it went.

The Marines spread out on the boat and they could hear them shouting about being pursued at sea, but the CIA agents were on the floor of the craft, exhausted from their flight. Now that they were at sea, they'd leave it to the Navy to keep them out of the clutches of the Turkish Mafia. On his knees from where he'd leapt onto the boat and dropped his prisoner, Trace had a couple of the Marines take their captive away. As they took the man below, Trace and Reed and Beau managed to get to their feet, watching the port of Mersin fade further and further away. In the wheelhouse, they could hear Marcos on the radio, relaying information about the capture.

Successful.

But, damn... by the skin of their teeth.

"Jesus," Beau grunted, looking for some place to sit down. "I thought we'd never make it."

He found a piece of equipment to perch his ass on and Trace followed him, sitting next to him.

"This is why we get paid the big bucks, boys," Trace said, wiping the sweat off his face. "And tomorrow, we'll do it all again."

"Not me," Beau said, shaking his head wearily. "This is my last one. Reed, too. We're done."

Trace knew that, but he didn't want to hear it. He was hoping they'd forgotten that both Beau and Reed were moving on from the CIA, something they'd both decided last year when a close friend had been killed in the line of fire. These hairy operations were what they did and they were very good at it, but Reed in particular wanted out. He had two young boys he wanted to see grow up, so Trace didn't blame him. Beau, too, was married and the woman spent most of her life alone.

But Trace? He was married. He had a young son. But it wasn't a marriage and he had no family life.

The CIA was his everything.

That was his curse.

"Well," Trace said after a moment. "We've got other guys in our group, but you two… I'm not just losing friends. I feel like I'm losing my brothers."

The boat bounced over the rough sea and they had to hold on or risk being tossed out. When the boat settled down, Beau turned to Trace.

"You're not losing us," he said. "You just won't be working with us. There's a time in every man's life when he has to evolve. Move on. It's our time to do that."

Trace shook his head. "I'm not there yet," he said. "I told Harry he's got me for good. He's happy."

Harry King was their supervisor, a brilliant man who managed these missions like a deadly game of chess. Trace, Reed, Beau, Marcos and the rest of the team were his knights, bishops, and pawns. In fact, Trace stood up and shouted to Marcos about contacting Harry and Marcos waved him off, signaling that he already had.

As the sea spray swirled around them and the American warship came into view, the men from the unit unofficially deemed the Unholy Angels knew that their time was drawing to a close. Their last mission together. Their last time together, as least as working colleagues.

Trace looked up at the pair of them.

"It's been a hell of a ride, boys," he said, reaching out to shake Beau's hand. "And a hell of a privilege."

Beau took the extended hand and held it tightly. "Same," he said. "We won't lose touch, Trace. Don't worry. We'll be keeping tabs on you and Marcos and the rest of the guys. Just know that if you need us – anytime, anywhere – we'll be here for you."

Trace smiled weakly. "Even with guns in the middle of Tajikistan?"

Beau snorted. "Probably not," he said. "But we'll wish you well. And... and take care of yourself, Trace. You're a crazy son-of-a-bitch sometimes. It would devastate me if something happened to you."

Trace chuckled softly. "Not me," he said. "I'm too much of a sinner to die. At least, that's what my mom says. She doesn't even know half of it."

Beau grinned, patting him on the shoulder as Reed came to him, his brown eyes glittering.

"We do," Reed said, shaking his hand. "We know the half and the whole of it and you *are* mortal, so no dying on us. Why not come up to Wyoming and work with me? My dad's got a spot for you."

"As a cop?" Trace said thoughtfully. Then, he shrugged. "Maybe. I think it's more than likely I'll end up with my dad's company."

"Building things?"

"Exactly. Far, far away from this shit."

He gestured to the ship around them. The death, the destruction, the chaos. They were closing in on the American vessel and Trace finally stood up, standing with Beau and Reed as they loomed closer. Soaking up the last few moments of this mission, of time spent with the best agents he'd ever worked with. It was a damn shame they were leaving the agency, but he understood.

He had to.

Not like he had a choice.

The small craft finally met up with the warship and after that, the men were too busy to discuss last missions or futures. It was all-business, even when they had dinner with the captain and crashed in their assigned bunks. The ship made it to Marseille, where Trace, Reed, Beau, and Marcos disembarked with their prisoner and were met by members of the US Embassy in France. They transferred their captive over to the justice department and, at that point, their orders were to fly back to Washington, DC.

Mission over.

And what a mission it had been.

In particular, they would remember drinking at the airport bar at de Gaulle before the flight home. The pledges that were made, the people that were slandered, and the amount of shots they did that caused those things. On the plane home, all they did was sleep and when they awoke in DC, it was to a new day, a new dynamic, and in the case of Beau and Reed, a new life. *All good things come to an end*, Trace said.

But not really.

They would always be the good guys and damn proud of it, but more than that, they formed a brotherhood like no other. Men that had faced danger and death together. There was no getting away from it.

Or each other.

The Unholy Angels were bonded for life.

PROLOGUE
HIGHWAY 80, JUST OUTSIDE OF JAMES TOWN, WYOMING, THE HI-WAY CAFÉ

WINTERS WERE BITTERLY cold this far north and this particular season had seen its share of sub-zero days. The Hi-Way Café, situated along a major east-west corridor through Southern Wyoming, seemed to invite a good deal of frozen truck drivers and weary travelers.

The building was old, immune to the cold with its thick, masonry walls because it had been a stage stop back in the days of the cowboys when outlaws and lawmen would roam the barren hills in search of both prey and shelter. The structure had a vibe about it that was simultaneously inviting and foreboding - it looked like it was off a studio back lot where the only people who entered it were those who were taken by mutants in the hills, never to be seen again.

It had been a bitterly cold night that had translated into a bitterly cold morning. Close to noon, the temperature was still flirting in the teens and the café had seen a lot of cold truck drivers crammed into its small dining room that morning, now cleared out because they all had some place to be. All that was left was some old hobo seated at the counter, a half-filled cup of coffee in front of him as his distant gaze stared off into nothingness.

It was the face of defeat.

But the employees didn't pay much attention to the tired old man as they went about their chores. Two cooks in the kitchen were prepping for the noon meal while the busboy, a local kid who worked more than forty hours a week to support his alcoholic mother, swept up the old, linoleum floor. The owner, a former truck driver with the smell of smoke and broken dreams about him, sat in the tiny and cluttered office talking on the phone to his shrew of a wife while the two waitresses wiped off tables and tidied up the dining room.

The older waitress was a brunette with eyes that went in different directions while the younger waitress, in her mid-thirties, looked sorely out of place. She was a beautiful woman in the midst of worn out and colorless surroundings. A few inches over five feet, she had a spectacular figure concealed beneath her plain white blouse and faded black work pants, and her long blonde hair was pulled back in a tight bun against the back of her head. She didn't wear much make-up and she usually had circles around her green eyes, but neither detracted from her stunning beauty.

No one knew much about her, however. She had shown up a year earlier and spent twelve hours sitting in one of the booths, drinking cup after cup of dark coffee, before the owner approached her and they struck up a conversation. Next thing he realized, he'd hired this mysterious and beautiful woman who went by the name of Clover. He paid her cash under the table and she seemed fine with that. She worked seventy hours, 7 days a week, for her five hundred dollars a week pay envelope, no questions asked.

The owner had never seen a more diligent worker. She was smart and knew how to deal appropriately with any customer. In fact, she had a lot of regulars who came around just to chat with her, but no one knew much more than her name. She never gave out any more information than that and when pressed, she would joke her way out of it. This elegant, sweet, intelligent woman was a complete enigma to the employees and customers of The Hi-Way Café.

With her portion of the restaurant cleaned up, Clover made her way back to the counter and began wiping it down. The old hobo, still staring off into space, lifted his cup when she passed by as if remembering to drink. It was too cold to go outside so he needed to pretend that he was still working on his coffee so they wouldn't kick him out. Clover, a rag in hand, finally glanced over at the old guy with the torn coat and heavy bag. Casually, she picked up the coffee pot and filled his cup back up to the rim. When he looked at her, she winked.

"Don't worry," she said softly. "You're not going anywhere. Just relax."

The old man smiled, displaying the only two teeth he had in his head. "It's sure cold out there."

Clover set the coffee pot back down on the warmer. "Yes, it is," she agreed, looking out of the windows at the snow-covered landscape beyond. "I've never seen a winter like this."

The old man sipped at his hot coffee. "I don't know what made me come to Wyoming," he said, looking over his shoulder at the same landscape she was looking at. "It seemed like a good idea at the time."

Clover grinned, showing off a spectacular smile. "That's what I thought when I came here. Now I'm not so sure."

The hobo turned to look at her. "Where are you from?"

Clover's smile faded. "Far away," she said. "Very far away. We don't have snow where I come from."

"Where's that?" the old man pressed, purely for the sake of conversation. "South?"

Clover nodded. "South," she said. "How about you? Where are you from?"

The hobo threw a thumb back over his shoulder, indicating one of a million directions. "Texas," he said. "Van Horn. Have you heard of it?"

Clover nodded, noticing that a sheriff's unit was pulling into their parking lot outside. "I've driven through it," she said. "I used to take road trips with my folks when I was a kid. My parents had an old tent trailer they used to pull around behind my dad's 1971 Ford Pinto. We camped in Van Horn once. There's not much there."

The old man lifted his bushy eyebrows as if to agree. "That's why I left."

He went back to sipping his coffee and Clover put her cleaning rag under the counter, moving to start another pot of coffee as a sheriff's deputy came inside. Bitter wind howled in after him, lifting the old vertical blinds on the windows nearest the door as he shut the panel behind him. Clover looked up from measuring coffee.

"Sit anywhere," she told the deputy.

The man nodded in thanks and lumbered towards the counter. He was bundled up in a regulation uniform and duty-issued cold weather jacket, fur-lined. He had heavy gloves on his hands, pulling them off as he approached the counter. The regulation cowboy hat came off next and he sat that, and the gloves, down on the old Formica counter. Clover alternately poured the water into the coffee machine and watched the deputy as he unzipped his coat.

"Coffee?" she asked him.

He nodded as he pulled off the jacket. "Please."

Clover finished pouring the water and flipped on the machine. Picking up a mug and a half-filled coffee pot that had been on a warmer, she went to the deputy and poured him a full cup as he slung his jacket over the back of the chair next to him.

As she poured, she began to notice just how big he was. He had enormous hands and, once the jacket came off, enormous arms and very broad shoulders. He was at least four or five inches over six feet and when she happened to glance at his face, she could see an extremely square jaw on his cold-pinched face. His dark hair was neatly cut and she was seriously checking him out as his bright blue eyes fixed on her.

"Thanks," he said as he sat heavily and picked up the coffee cup.

"You're welcome," she said, tearing her gaze off of him as she set the coffee pot back on the warmer. "Do you want to see a menu or do you know what you want?"

He sipped at his very hot coffee. "Do you have a BLT sandwich?"

Clover nodded. "On white or wheat?"

"Wheat."

"French fries or fruit?"

"Fruit. Can I also get a salad with that?"

"Ranch, Italian, honey-mustard, or bleu cheese?"

"Italian."

"You got it."

Clover turned around and picked up her ticket book, writing the order down and posting it for the cook. Then she went to go fill up a glass of water for the deputy and a second one for the hobo. She set the glass down in front of the old man first and then two chairs down the counter, set the second glass in front of the deputy.

"Busy out there today?" she asked the man pleasantly.

He pulled a couple of Advil out of his pocket, giving her a half-grin. "A little," he said. "Hopefully the rest of the day will be calm." He thumped on the counter in a "knock on wood" gesture.

Clover grinned at him. "Then I wish you luck," she

said, her gaze lingering on him for a moment. "We haven't seen you around here. Are you new?"

He tossed back the Advil and drank the entire glass of water to chase it. "No," he said, shaking his head and wiping his mouth. "I'm not from Sweetwater County. I'm from up north in Fremont."

She cocked her head. "You're a ways from home."

He nodded and collected his coffee cup. His blue eyes were fixed on her, perhaps studying her as if he just realized how cute she really was. In fact, his entire manner softened a little as his piercing gaze seemed to study every contour of her face.

"A little ways," he concurred quietly. "I'm just heading back from some business in Salt Lake City."

"I see," Clover said, noticing over his shoulder that another car was pulling into the parking lot. It was a beat-up four door sedan but she didn't pay any more attention than that. "Well, drive safe, deputy. The roads are icy right now."

He sighed wearily. "No kidding," he said. "I've already come across two accidents this morning. I've spent the past hour helping clear one a couple of miles west of here."

"Then I'll keep the coffee coming. You must be half-frozen."

"You could probably light me on fire right now and I wouldn't feel it."

Clover laughed softly, not really having too much more to say, but her smile was warm. He returned the smile. She turned away, still grinning, thinking that the man made her feel the least bit giddy. He was damn good looking and that baritone voice bubbling up from his toes had her heart racing just a little.

In the cook's window, his sandwich and salad were waiting so she collected them both and placed them carefully in front of him just as three young men entered the restaurant. They were all bundled up against the cold, which was normal, so Clover didn't give them a second look as she picked up some extra napkins for the deputy and put them by his coffee cup. She was moving to refill his water glass when one young man threw off his heavy coat and produced a gun.

"Everybody stay put," he ordered, the gun pointing right at the deputy's back. "Sheriff, if you turn around, I'm gonna blow your head off. Understand?"

The deputy froze, as did Clover and the hobo. The other waitress, who had been coming to the front of the restaurant from the kitchen door, shrieked when she saw the gun, causing one of the young men to run over and grab her. He forced her into a chair as she screamed and he brought out another gun from his belt and pointed it right at her.

"Shut up!" he yelled at her.

The waitress buried her face in her hands and wept. The third young man, tall and skinny and nervous, rushed at the cash register. He had a grocery bag in his hand.

"You!" he threw a finger at Clover. "Open this!"

Clover did as she was told. She was surprisingly cool as she moved to the register, entered a "no sale", and the drawer popped open. The skinny kid waved a sharp hand at her.

"Back off," he ordered.

She did, going back to her original position in front of the deputy. Meanwhile, the deputy calmly set his sandwich down and put his hands on the counter where they were in plain sight. He kept his gaze focused on Clover. She met his gaze with little fear in her expression. She mostly looked concerned. She was a cool woman, not one to go crazy with fright. As the deputy gazed at her, he could see that innate control and it impressed him. There was something about her that was magnetic and calm, even under fire. Had he not been so concerned for what was going on behind him, he would have found her demeanor utterly fascinating.

"Sorry we gotta do this," the first young man with the gun said. "Times are tough for everybody. Nobody move and you'll all live through this."

The employees and patrons of the grill didn't say a word. The first young man moved closer, keeping the gun trained on the deputy's broad back. His nervous gaze moved over the restaurant, seeking out anything else he could steal. He passed over the hobo and went straight to Clover.

"You gotta safe in the back?" he asked.

Clover nodded steadily. "There's one in the office," she said. "But it was emptied last night. There won't be any more money in it until the end of the workday."

The young man looked at her as if he didn't believe

her. Then he looked at the deputy. "Stand up, Sheriff," he commanded.

Slowly, the deputy stood up, still facing Clover. His gaze never left her and Clover gazed back at him, silently imparting her encouragement to him. But he didn't seem to need it. There was more than calmness in his gaze - there was utter control, concern for his situation, and perhaps some scheming going on, as if he were planning his big move to see them all safely out of this predicament. Clover could see his determination in his face. The man was going to make it out of there alive. He kept his hands where they could be seen as the young man with the gun came to within a few feet of him, the barrel of the gun pointing at the middle of his back.

"Take your gun belt off," the young man told him. "Let it fall to the ground."

The deputy unhooked his Sam Browne and the entire belt fell to the ground, service weapon included. Once that was done, the young man with the gun walked up behind him and pistol-whipped him on the back of the head.

The deputy fell like a stone.

The waitress with her face in her hands screamed at the violent action. Even Clover jumped, horrified at the sight of the deputy now motionless on the floor. The robber who had been watching the waitress ran into the kitchen and emerged a few moments later with the cooks, the busboy, and the owner, everyone with their hands up. He grouped them all near the weeping waitress.

"Hurry up," he told the skinny kid collecting the last of the money from the register. "We need to get out of here."

The skinny kid had his money, or at least all that was in the register. He began rifling through the candy at the counter, throwing that in the bag as well, as the first robber with the gun stood over the unconscious deputy. He reached down and unsnapped the man's service holster, pulling forth the service revolver. He looked it over.

"This is nice," he said. "I may have to keep this."

At his feet, the deputy stirred, and he pointed the service weapon at the man's head as he came around.

"Don't get up," he told the man. Then, he sighed heavily. "See, now? I told you not to look at me and you did. Now you know my face."

Clover, still rooted to the spot, could see the deputy's groggy expression as he gazed up at the robber. Even so, there was no fear there whatsoever, but Clover was feeling a good deal of apprehension. She didn't like what the robber said or the way he said it. It led her to believe that the deputy was in danger, much more than the rest of them. The robber was zeroed in on the man's badge and what he represented. She could already see it wasn't going to go well for him.

At her feet at the base of the counter, tucked in under the lip of the bottom shelf, was a loaded rifle. The owner always kept it there for times such as this. In fact, he'd been robbed three times in the past year alone. Being a lonely stop on a lonely highway, they got their share of shifty characters. Clover had always known the gun was there but she'd never had to get near it much less use it. Still, she couldn't let the robber shoot the deputy in cold blood. She knew that was where it was headed simply by the way the robber was speaking. Her training, from her past life, told her as much. Once, very long ago, she had dealt with people like this on a daily basis. She knew she had to gain the upper hand and she had to get that deputy off the ground. If she didn't, things were going to be very bad, indeed.

"What am I supposed to do now?" the first robber said, bent over the supine deputy. "If you saw my face, then you can identify me and I don't want to go to jail. So what am I supposed to do?"

He pointed the service revolver at the deputy's face. The deputy didn't flinch as he looked down the barrel of his own gun.

"Right now, you'd just be held for armed robbery," he said evenly. "If you kill me, it'll be murder and Wyoming is a capital punishment state. Robbery will get you ten years, maybe less. It's really your choice if you want to die by lethal injection or just spend the next ten years in prison."

The robber shook his head sadly. "If you aren't around to identify me, then I can't get caught," he said, a ludicrous statement considering everyone in the restaurant had seen him. "I'm gonna have to kill you."

"You need to reconsider that action."

He said it so calmly, as if discussing the weather. Meanwhile, the skinny kid who had stolen all the money and candy was now rifling through the gift shop items they had on a shelf, stealing little knick-knacks. The second robber with a gun was holding the weapon on the cooks, owner, and the other waitress. His attention was diverted by the owner, who was trying to talk him out of robbing him. Only Clover and the hobo weren't being closely watched and she knew she had to move. It was now or never while everyone was diverted. She wouldn't have a second chance.

Under the radar, she reached out and collected the deputy's empty water glass on the counter in front of her. Making sure that the robbers' attention was still elsewhere, she threw the glass as hard as she could at the front door. As it exploded against the doorframe, she hit the floor and grabbed the rifle behind the counter. She rolled to her knees, using the counter as a shield, and fired off a well-aimed shot at the first robber, hitting him squarely in the torso.

The first robber launched backwards with the force of the blow, hitting the old linoleum floor in an explosion of blood as the deputy's service revolver flew out of his hand and landed not too far from where the deputy was still on his back. But before the deputy could get to his weapon, Clover expended the used shell and turned the rifle on the second robber with the gun. He was running toward her and managed to peel off a shot that ruptured the coffee machine behind her. Clover deftly ducked it, cocked the rifle, and got off a second well-aimed blast that hit the second robber in the head.

His skull exploded, sending blood and tissue everywhere. Meanwhile, the deputy was up with his revolver in his hand, pointing it at the third robber, who was, by now, screaming that he didn't want to die. He threw the money bag on the ground and lifted his hands into the air, begging the deputy not to shoot him. Behind him, the deputy could hear Clover cocking the rifle again and he threw up a hand to stop her.

"No more," he told her, his focus on the quivering robber, now down on his knees. "It's all over."

Clover held the rifle with a rock-steady grip, the sights on the sobbing robber. She just stood there, holding it, her finger on the trigger as if waiting for the man to make a wrong move so she could take his head off, too.

So many thoughts and memories suddenly flashed before her eyes at that moment, things she hadn't thought of in a year. A full year of distancing herself from the hell that she had run from. Memories flashed through her mind of her husband and of a little boy and girl giggling at her, calling her "mommy". Then there was her job, a badge on her chest, her assignment to the Los Angeles Sheriff's Department Gang Taskforce that took six years of her life.

Commendations. Arrests. Trials.

More flashbacks. A man with the gang moniker of Mickey Mouse with a teardrop tattooed on his face telling her that she would live to regret the day she was born. She didn't believe him, of course, until her husband was driving the children to school in her car one day and Mickey Mouse and his friends were lying in wait a block from the school.

Ambush. Blood. Death.

Her life was over.

The rifle fell out of her hands. She was whirling blindly for the kitchen door, bolting through it as the deputy called after her. She had her car keys in her pocket because she always kept them with her and her car was parked back behind the grill. She jumped in the car without her purse or any of her identification and tore off in the direction of Green River, a little town where she rented a little one-bedroom trailer for two hundred dollars a month, month to month.

She cleaned out the little home in twenty-seven minutes and then she was back on the road again, leaving everything behind just as she had done before. She didn't care about the possessions. She only cared about getting away. Her fragile heart and fragile mind couldn't handle anything else. She knew if she had remained with the deputy and gave a police report about the incident at the Hi-Way, that they would need her real name and once she gave that, it would all come out. The truth. Then she couldn't hide from it anymore.

She couldn't face the truth. She had to keep running.

ONE
THREE YEARS LATER, THE MONTH OF JUNE, RIVERTON, WYOMING

AT THE TAIL end of a twelve-hour shift he wasn't even supposed to be working, the last call before he went home was an unwelcome delay between him and his mattress. All he wanted to do was go home and sleep. Hell, this wasn't even his city but he was on a mutual aid call. Exhaustion fed his irritation as he pulled the sheriff's unit up in front of a row of restored brick buildings that had been built back at the turn of the nineteenth century.

He grunted as he wearily climbed out of the car, securing his baton. Then he pulled out his hat, a regulation uniform cowboy hat that was expensive and pristine, and put it on his dark head. Bright blue eyes glanced up at the sky as the morning deepened, noting it was going to be another hot and dry day. They saw a lot of those this far north in Wyoming, the curse of the high plains summer that could leave them hot and dusty one day, wet and muggy the next.

As he closed the car door, muffling the chatter on the radio, he made his way onto the curb. The call had been from the trendiest restaurant in town, or so his dad had told him, and he took a moment to inspect the exterior. The *Coffee Cakery* it said. His mom and dad apparently loved the place, but this was the first time he'd come here. He was only back in Riverton because his dad had assigned him to the substation in Lander. As Sheriff of Fremont County, his dad had the right to assign his deputies anywhere they were needed.

That meant that he was back in the town he'd grown up in, a place he didn't particularly like hanging out in. But he knew the town like the back of his hand, which made him particularly effective when it came to law enforcement and public safety. Still, he didn't like being here. Too many memories. With thoughts of hurrying through this call, he made his way inside the crowded, fragrant restaurant.

A pretty, young hostess tried to kick people off of the counter for him until he insisted he wasn't there to eat but to work. The girl with the big, fake, pink nails and a nose piercing had no idea what he was talking about, calling over one of the waiters, who went in search of the manager. The manager seemed to know what the call was about and gestured for him to follow. He ended up following the man all the way into the back of the restaurant as the manager called in to the open office in the back.

"Kinley," he said in a heavy Mexican accent. "The deputy is here."

The manager excused himself as a figure emerged from the open office. The deputy found himself gazing into green eyes with a fringe of dark lashes. He felt an odd sensation as he gazed into them, like an electrical current, and he soon realized that he recognized the face belonging to the eyes. Long ago, on a winter's day, those eyes had saved his life. He was so startled that his mouth actually popped open.

"It... it's *you!*" he hissed.

Kinley Connors-Berrington recognized the deputy, too. The granite-square jaw and bright blue eyes were an instant giveaway, stirring memories long buried. She stumbled back, her mouth open and her eyes wide.

"Oh... oh, God," she gasped, grabbing at the doorframe. "It's... you from the...."

The deputy took a step towards her, hardly realizing that he was moving. He was in a complete state of astonishment, shocked to the bone to see someone he never honesty thought he'd see again. In his excitement, he came on like a bull in a china shop. With his size and booming voice, he could be intimidating and forceful whether or not he wanted to be.

"Do you remember me?" he asked. "Jesus Ch... this is amazing. Do you work here?"

Kinley was still holding on to the door frame, looking at him with big eyes. But those eyes quickly filled with tears and the joy and surprise on the deputy's face disappeared when he saw how upset she was. He realized that he must have come across much stronger than he had intended, but his surprise had been great. It still was. He held up his hands in a soothing gesture.

"I'm sorry," he said quickly, quietly. "I didn't mean to upset you. But, seriously... I've been looking for you for two years and..."

Kinley turned away from him, swiftly, retreating into the office and trying to shut the door. "Please... please just go away," she said tightly. "Forget you saw me."

The deputy wedged himself in the doorway so she couldn't close the door but stopped short of entering. He could see how shook up she was and, if he thought hard about it, he knew why. She had fled the crime scene those years ago in a panic and they'd been unable to find her. She probably thought she was in some kind of trouble and that he was here to deliver the bad news. He hastened to reassure her.

"I'm sorry," he said again, more gently. "I didn't mean to scare you. I'm just surprised to see you, that's all. I've been looking for you for three years and here you were all the time."

By this time, Kinley was behind her desk, using it as a barrier between them. She looked as if she were about to jump out of the window.

"Would you please go?" she whispered nervously.

He sighed heavily, realizing she wasn't going to be an easy sell. She was defensive and frightened, and he felt badly.

"Look," he said, lowering his voice. "You don't have to

be frightened. You're not in any trouble or anything. I've been looking for you because I wanted to thank you."

Kinley was still stiff with apprehension. She wiped at her brimming eyes. "I... I don't know what you mean."

He held up a finger, begging silently for her patience, as he retrieved his wallet and began rifling through it. Then he pulled out what looked like a business card and set it carefully on her desk, facing her. Then he stepped back to a safe distance as she peered cautiously at the piece of paper. When she realized what it was, her face went slack with surprise - it was the driver license she had left behind three years ago when she fled the Hi-Way Café. Now, astonishment joined the other emotions on her face as she looked up at him.

The deputy smiled timidly.

"It says your name is Clover Fields," he said quietly. "We searched high and low for you but never came close to finding you. It was as if you had disappeared into thin air. I get that Clover isn't your real name and, frankly, I really don't care. I just wanted to thank the woman that saved my life and nothing more. Now that I've found you, I'm just very happy and relieved that I finally get to thank you face to face. That's all there is to it."

Kinley stared down at the falsified driver license with her picture on it. She just stared at it, silently, as the deputy lingered by the door. For the longest time, she just looked at the identification and he just stood there, not moving a muscle. Then, she reached down and picked the license up, looking at it at close range.

"You've been driving around with this in your wallet all this time?" she asked hoarsely.

He nodded firmly. "I have," he said. "It reminds me daily of how lucky I was when my guardian angel intervened."

Kinley looked up at him sharply. There wasn't any emotion in his face other than warmth. The bright blue eyes were glittering at her and she could feel that odd magnetic pull between them, the same pull she had felt three years ago when they had first met. Her gaze lingered on him a moment.

"I don't even know your name," she finally said.

"Reed," he said without hesitation. "Reed McCoy."

Kinley's gaze lingered on him a moment longer before sitting slowly in her chair. She finally put the license down. "Wow," she murmured. "I... I don't even know what to say right now."

He took a step or two into the office. "Well," he said thoughtfully, "you can tell me why you called the sheriff's department."

She looked up at him, confused. "Come again?"

He grinned. "You called the cops, lady," he said. "I'm the responding officer. How can I help you today?"

She looked at him, realizing he wasn't there to bust her, or yell at her, or anything else. She'd completely forgotten the fact that she'd called the sheriff's department until he reminded her. The shock of seeing him had wiped that little detail from her mind. But now, realizing that there was no reason for her to be nervous or upset around him, she forced herself to calm. It was a struggle.

She set the driver license back on the desk.

"Right," she said, giving him a weak smile as she shifted her focus. Why *had* she called the sheriff's department? "It seems that my employees are getting parking tickets on their cars when they park in the back of the restaurant and are there for over six hours. I told your desk officer that when I called but he said I needed to come into the station. I told him that I needed someone to come out and see what I'm talking about so we can come to a resolution. I can't have my employees getting parking tickets in our own lot."

His gaze lingered on her. "You own this place?"

"I lease the building and opened the restaurant nineteen months ago."

He nodded, silently pulling out his pad of paper from his back pocket. Producing a pen, he jotted down a few notes.

"Your name?" he asked.

Kinley hesitated, waiting for him to say something about her real name and not the fake moniker of Clover Fields. That was all he knew her as. But he was focused on his pad of paper, pen poised, waiting for her to speak.

"Kinley Connors-Berrington," she finally said. "Connors with two 'n's. It's hyphenated with the Berrington."

"Address?"

"Can I just use the restaurant address?"

"If you want to."

"605 East Main Street."

"Phone number?"

"307-202-1559."

After he finished writing down the information, he turned on his heel and headed out of her office and to the back door of the restaurant. Kinley followed him out into the parking lot, standing quietly as he wrote down the municipal codes on the parking signs in the lot. She was more at ease with his presence now as he shifted into professional mode, giving her a chance to calm down after their shocking introduction.

In fact, she found herself watching him closely, remembering the size of the man and his muscular build, and thinking that he had gotten more handsome over the past few years. There was a little salt and pepper on his temples now. He had the squarest jaw she'd ever seen, like the ones drawn in comic books for superhero characters. She watched him as he walked around the lot, looking at the cars, the parking situation, and jotted down a few notes. Still writing, he made his way back over to her.

"How many employees do you have?" he asked.

"Anywhere from eight to fourteen depending on the day and the shift," she replied.

He finished writing and looked at her. "You're going to have to get parking permits for your employees for anything over four hours," he told her. "The municipal code doesn't allow for anything over that."

She looked at the big, metal black and white sign behind her. "They just put these signs up a little while ago," she said, returning her focus to him. "I guess there *has* been a lot of traffic since I opened."

He looked around at the adjacent businesses. "My guess is that someone called the department to complain," he said. "Your business is successful and you've got a lot of people parking all over the place. That tends to piss the lesser-busy businesses off."

She made a face. "Business-envy is a terrible thing."

He grinned, showing off his big, white teeth and perfect smile. "I have news for you, Ms. Berrington," he said. "Anyone and everyone are going to be envious of you, so you'd better get used to it."

She smiled reluctantly. "I've been very lucky," she replied humbly. "The cakery has taken off and I feel very fortunate."

He nodded, glancing back at the rear of the restaurant. "My parents love it. They come here all of the time."

Kinley cocked her head curiously. "Your parents live around here?"

He nodded. "I grew up here. My parents still live in the house I grew up in."

Her smile turned genuine. "You didn't go far, did you?"

He was enjoying the fact that she was finally relaxing around him, enough to the point where the conversation was turning casual. He was thrilled.

"Actually, I was in Washington D.C. for quite a while," he told her. "I only returned about three years ago."

"What did you do in D.C.?"

"Naval Investigative Services and then the CIA for a while."

Her eyebrows rose. "You were in the CIA?"

"For about ten years."

Her gaze was warm on him. "Then being a small-town deputy is a piece of cake."

He chuckled. "Sometimes," he agreed. "But sometimes it's worse. Lots of land out here. Lots of things can happen. I think I've been in more dicey situations here than I ever was back in D.C."

Like robbery in a small diner. Kinley's smile faded as her thoughts came around again to the first time they met. It was hard not to think about it. Meanwhile, Reed put his pad and pen away, and they began to walk back towards the restaurant's back door. He couldn't help but notice she'd fallen silent. His gaze moved over the exposed brick façade of the rear of the business.

"When I was a kid, a lot of these buildings were derelict," he said, making conversation because of the swift downturn in the mood. "The bums lived around here. Now, it's the fashionable part of town. I still find that weird sometimes."

Kinley forced a smile as they entered the back door into the fragrant confines of the restaurant. "I'll bet," she said. "Have you had breakfast? Do you want to take something with you to go?"

He looked at her, seeing an opportunity in her softly uttered words. He was attracted to her the moment he'd met her. In just those few short words after their introduction, in those few brief seconds, he had felt a pull towards her as he'd never felt toward anyone. Sure, she'd run off after the shooting, but he had attributed that to panic until he'd come across her driver's license and had discovered it to be false.

After that, he'd entertained all sorts of wild ideas. A fugitive, a criminal, a spy...all kinds of things had entered his head. She'd used that rifle with a hell of a lot of skill and an ice-cold demeanor, which was an acquired talent. But the fact remained that none of those thoughts could dampen the attraction he felt toward her. There was a spark there just dying to be kindled. The woman was running from something. He wanted to know what it was and he wanted to know her on a personal level.

He couldn't explain it more than that.

"My parents say you have fantastic Bananas Foster French toast," he said. "Maybe I should judge for myself."

Kinley's smile turned real. "To eat here or to go?"

His gaze lingered on her. He was supposed to be off watch and his mattress was calling to him. But that didn't seem to matter at the moment.

"Here," he replied. "But I have a favor to ask."

"What's that?"

"Can I have my good luck charm back? I left it on your desk."

His French toast order came with a side of an envelope

containing the driver's license with a pirate's beard, Hitler mustache, and eye-patch colored over the picture in heavy black ink so anyone looking at it couldn't make out who the person really was. But in his eyes, it still couldn't detract from the unearthly beauty beneath.

He just sat there and grinned.

TWO

KINLEY WAS at the restaurant the next day at four in the morning to get ready for the breakfast rush. It was Saturday, usually her busiest day, so the line cooks and sous chef were busy preparing for the onslaught. When the doors opened at six, there were already people waiting outside and the restaurant was half-full within minutes.

Unfortunately, two of her servers called in sick so Kinley stepped in to take orders. She had several regulars, people she spent a good deal of time chatting with in between placing and serving breakfast orders. As the sun rose, the Coffee Cakery was warm and fragrant, alive with people coming and going for breakfast. By eight in the morning, it was packed solid and the scent of coffee edged out the scent of cinnamon. The hip eatery on the east side of town was in full swing.

Kinley called in a couple of off duty servers to fill in the shifts and was able to get off the floor by mid-morning. Still, she hung around at the lunch counter, chatting with customers and making sure everyone was generally satisfied. All the while, she kept watching the cars out of the big storefront driving up and down Main Street. When she'd see a sheriff's unit, her heart would jump a little. It took her a while to figure out that she was waiting for Reed McCoy to make an appearance. At least, she was hoping he would.

As much as he frightened her and as much as she didn't want to admit it, she was glad he had returned yesterday. He stirred feelings within her that she hadn't felt in years. It was wholly terrifying but utterly wonderful. Still, she was leaning toward the side of caution. She knew she wasn't ready for an emotional attachment of any kind. It was safer if she didn't.

So, she left the counter, and the chatty customers, and headed back to her office to do some work. Her office door was next to the rear entrance to the restaurant and she stood at the open door a moment, gazing out into the full parking lot and seeing Reed in her mind's eye as he walked around and wrote in his notepad. He cut quite a figure in his khaki-drab uniform and cowboy hat. Shutting the back door, she pushed him from her mind.

The day moved on and the breakfast rush moved into the lunch rush. The restaurant only served breakfast and lunch, so there was standing room only as noon rolled around. The hostess was swamped, the manager was back in the kitchen helping with orders, so Kinley finished up the invoices she was working on in the office and went to the front of the house to help with the cash register. The place was hopping and somewhere in the back, a cook had burned toast so the smell of burned bread filled the air. Everything was bustling and the sound of the cash register chiming was filling the air.

The hostess returned from her duties to help with the cash register, but as Kinley moved back to the hallway where her office was, she could see that several orders were up. The servers were efficient but one had a particularly large order, so Kinley collected three lunches for table eighteen and headed out for the patio that fronted the main street. She smiled as she approached table eighteen with three people.

"Hello, there," she said. The way the orders were written on the ticket ensured that she already knew who got what order. She deftly slid the big veggie burger plate down in front of a middle-aged gentleman. "Here's your veggie burger and salad. And for you, ma'am," she sat a big Cobb salad down in front of the attractive middle-aged woman with short, dark hair, "your lovely salad. And last but not least, a BLT with fruit for..."

Her eyes fell on the third person in the party. She hadn't paid any attention until now, realizing as she set that plate down that Reed was gazing up at her. Dressed in street clothes, including worn cowboy boots, he looked like he had just stepped off the pages of a magazine. He was hunky, relaxed, and all shades of dreamy in the mid-morning sunshine. He had a lazy half-smile on his face as their gazes locked.

"You sure have the best French toast in town," he said, his eyes twinkling. "Let's see how the BLT is."

Over her initial surprise, Kinley couldn't help but smile. "Hello," she said. "I didn't see you slip in."

There were four chairs at the table. He slung his big arm over the back of the empty chair that happened to be between them. The way he did it was just inviting her to sit down and be a part of that casual embrace.

"I didn't see you when we came in, either," he said. His eyes never left her face. "These are my parents, Harmon and Shirley McCoy. They're the ones in love with your restaurant."

Kinley turned to the pair, shaking Harmon's hand and then Shirley's. "I'm so glad," she said. "I'm Kinley Berrington. People like you are keeping me in business."

Harmon was already into his food. "You don't need our help," he said, mouth full. "Keep cooking like this and you'll do just fine."

Kinley grinned, bright and beautiful. "Well, thanks," she said, glancing at Reed, who had yet to even look at his food. He was staring at her, swallowing her up with his big blue eyes. "Is that all you ever eat? BLT sandwiches?"

He laughed softly, finally breaking his stare to glance down at his big, beautiful sandwich. "I've got a thing for bacon, I admit it," he said. "What about you? Do you eat at all?"

"Sometimes."

"Can you join us for a minute, then?" Reed asked,

pulling out the empty chair. "I'll even share my bacon with you."

Kinley looked at him and then at the chair. Her first instinct was that she very much wanted to sit but then her second, more powerful, instinct told her not to. They would make small talk and conversation, and eventually ask her about herself. She didn't want to talk about herself, not in the least. She hated to be rude because instinct already had her warming to these people, but her sense of self-protection won out.

"I'm sorry, I can't," she said, backing away. "We're really busy right now. But it was good to see you all. Please come back again."

With that, she turned on her heel and fled before Reed could say another word. As his parents dug into their food with gusto, he was still watching Kinley until she disappeared from sight. She had been polite enough, and there was something in her expression that suggested warmth. It was that same natural warmth he'd seen the first time they met at the Hi-Way Café, sort of an underlying sincerity that was both mysterious and attractive. She seemed outgoing enough but wary of something more than cursory conversation. Still, he sensed something far more to the woman, something deep.

He had from the first.

As he turned to his BLT, he decided he was going to find out what more he could about her. He'd thought about it briefly yesterday after learning her real name, but he'd refrained from doing any research simply because it was an invasion of privacy. He wasn't a stalker. But he was very, very interested in the woman who saved his life. Maybe if he ran a general search on the internet, he could find out a little something about her. *Kinley Connors-Berrington.*

After lunch, he went to the Riverton Sheriff Station to do some investigating.

THREE

"BACK AGAIN?"

Reed heard the question and glanced up from the computer. He was seated in the report writing office used by the deputies when filing their paperwork, a room that smelled of cigarette smoke, disinfectant, and leather. The carpet was old and worn, a testament to the lawmen that had walked the floors over the years, him and his father included.

He pulled off his reading glasses as the deputy who asked the question entered the room. "We don't need you here," the deputy said. "You've already got half the women in town flooding dispatch wanting to know who the good-looking new deputy is."

Reed grinned, leaning back in his chair and rubbing his eyes. "Oh, yeah?" he said. "What are you telling them?"

"That you're a heartbreaker who's been married eight

times and has a dozen kids," the deputy said, laughing. "Besides, you're not new."

Reed shook his head. "I've been in the Lander substation for years," he said. "Hell, before yesterday, I've barely been to Riverton the past three years even though my folks live here. I was born here. But I have no desire to spend any time here."

The deputy lifted his eyebrows. "So you'd rather stay in that backward town of Lander?"

Reed shrugged. "It's good for me," he said quietly. "I've got my spread outside of town, my horses and livestock to keep me happy. Being back in Riverton just brings... memories."

Deputy Steve Turner just shook his head. A big man with a shaved head, he had the dark eyes and high cheekbones to go along with his half-Shoshone blood.

"Bad ones?"

"Bad enough."

"What in the hell are you talking about?" Steve asked, slapping him on the shoulder. "You were king of the high school – home-coming king, king of the football team, king of everything. I oughta know. I spent all those years in your shadow. And then you ran off to D.C. to be in the Navy or something."

"I didn't 'run off' to be in the Navy," Reed clarified. "I had a scholarship to Annapolis and joined the Marines. After that, it was the CIA. It was a better life for me there, away from this town. Away from... stuff."

Steve cocked his head. He knew exactly what Reed meant. They'd been friends since grade school and there wasn't much they didn't know about each other.

"You had to get away from memories of Heather," he said after a moment.

Reed's good humor fled completely and he averted his gaze. "It's not every prom king who kills his queen right before graduation."

Steve lost some of his aggressive demeanor. "You didn't kill her," he said quietly. "You were hit by a drunk driver. Twenty years down the road, don't you even get that?"

Reed sighed heavily and pretended to focus on the computer again. "I do," he said. "But it's something I pushed from my mind for all of those years. I just don't like to think about it, especially when I pass by her street on my way to visit my folks. My dad told me her parents still live in that blue house with the white shutters."

"They do," Steve said. "They never blamed you. I still don't get why you blame yourself."

Reed shrugged and put his reading glasses back on. "I don't know," he said, looking at the screen. "I guess I just need to get over it."

"You were married for a while once you moved to D.C., weren't you? Didn't that make you get over it?"

Reed sighed. "It made the pain go away but not the sadness," he said. "It was kind of a disaster, you know. I went around looking for women that looked just like Heather and ended up marrying one. It only lasted eight years, and I was away on tours or other things for half of those."

"You have kids, too."

"Two boys. They live with their mother on the east coast. I get them during the summer."

He didn't sound too happy. Mostly, he sounded resigned, like this was his life now and it would never be anything better. Steve slapped him on the back again.

"Well," he said. "It's time for you to move on. You're a big boy now, Reed. Stop clinging to the past."

Reed nodded his head, faintly. "You're right," he said. "But I still hate this town."

"We hate you, too."

Reed grinned, shaking off the depression that threatened. He didn't want to deal with it today, the constant shadow that had been his companion since that dark May night many years ago. It was the first time he'd spoken of it for years, mostly because it was something he kept buried deep. He didn't like to talk about the high school sweetheart who ended up being buried on the day she should have graduated from high school. He still didn't like to talk about it, now almost angry with Steve for bringing it up. Forcibly, he lightened his mood.

"Don't you have something you should be doing?" he asked. "Like shuttling little kids across the crosswalk? Go bother someone else. I'm busy."

Steve made a face at him. "Just because you worked for the government doesn't mean you're such a bad-ass," he said, plopping next to Reed and noticing that he was doing something on the computer. "What are you doing?"

Reed was fixed on a particular website, trying to read as Steve chattered. "Looking something up."

"What?"

Reed didn't mind telling him; oddly enough, Steve wasn't a gossip. He could keep his mouth shut when necessary. For some reason, Reed found the need to confide in someone he trusted. He was actually somewhat excited about the end to a very long search.

"Do you remember that shooting at a restaurant I was involved in down in Green River about two years ago?" he asked. "The one with three robbery suspects and two of them were killed?"

Steve looked thoughtful. "I do," he said slowly. "I don't remember too much about it, though. Why?"

Reed looked at him. "I was sitting at the lunch counter, on-duty, when the three suspects entered," he said, lowering his voice. "To make a long story short, they went after me pretty good and I'm positive they were going to kill me, but one of the waitresses saved my life. She got a hold of a rifle behind the counter and capped two of the suspects, particularly the one who had my service weapon and was about to blow my brains out. Before help arrived, or before I could even thank her, she ran off and disappeared."

Steve nodded as he began to recall more of the story. "I seem to remember your dad saying something about the waitress who saved your ass," he said. "You never did find her, did you?"

Reed shrugged, glancing back at the computer screen. "She left behind her purse which contained her identification, but we quickly found out it was fraudulent," he said. "All I knew was that her name was Clover Fields, but Clover Fields didn't exist anywhere. For three years I've been carrying around her fake I.D. like... like Prince Charming carrying around Cinderella's glass slipper, hunting for a woman who vanished into thin air. Yesterday, I finally found her."

Steve's eyebrows lifted. "You *found* her?" he repeated. "Where?"

Reed's eyes were twinkling somewhat. "At that restaurant everyone in town is crazy about – the Coffee Cakery."

"That place?" Steve said, incredulous. "I go there all of the time. Who is she?"

"The owner," Reed replied. "I went on a call there yesterday and had to take a report, so she had to give me her real name - Kinley Connors-Berrington."

Steve was surprised. "Wow," he said. "That's a pretty amazing story. Did she recognize you?"

Reed nodded. "She did," he said. "It freaked her out at first, but she calmed down. I think she thought she was in trouble for fleeing the scene. I told her she wasn't in any trouble. After all this time, there's no reason to get into that again. I'm sure she had her reasons for running off."

"She was scared."

"Exactly," Reed agreed, returning his attention to the

computer. "But there was more to it than that, I think. She was using a fake I.D., so I thought maybe she was a fugitive or in the witness protection program. People don't use fake I.D.'s for no reason. Plus, she handled a gun like she was trained on it. The way she got those shots off... it was impressive."

Steve was starting to follow his line of thought. "So now that you know her real name, what did you find out about her?"

Reed was reading the computer screen. "I've had to run a few different spelling versions," he said. "Nothing is really popping up except Scottish heritage websites or plumbers."

"Nothing about her yet?"

Reed shook his head and tried another version of her name. "Even though she signed the report I took yesterday, it's hard to make out the spelling. So let me try... this."

He hit the return key and they both watched the page populate. Several website listings popped up, but one in particular was highlighted at the top of the page. They both peered closer at what they saw.

"Los Angeles Sheriff's Department?" Steve was the first to read aloud.

Reed brought up a website related to Kinley's name and they were both intensely curious when her picture, in a neat Los Angeles County Sheriff's uniform, popped up along with the article. Steve's first reaction was the obvious.

"Hey," he pointed at the picture. "Is that her?"

Reed was glued to the image. "It sure is."

"She's really hot."

"You have no idea."

Moving past the picture, they began to decipher the article. The more they read, the more shocked their expressions became. By the time they hit the end of the article, Reed's mouth was hanging open.

He couldn't help it.

"Oh... my God," he breathed.

FOUR

IT WAS six o'clock in the evening and Kinley was finally leaving the restaurant. She and her manager, plus the executive chef, had been going over the supplies because the chef was changing the menu to reflect more of what the local farmers produced, so they were working on finalizing the menu change. Kinley was all about sustainable, local suppliers. Still, the day had been long and exhausting. She was looking forward to going home and crashing on the couch.

It was still relatively hot and dry outside as she locked the back door, indicative of the high plains weather she had been forced by necessity to get used to. Her non-descript Toyota sedan was waiting for her at the edge of the parking lot. She'd thought about getting a new car but she liked this one because it didn't make her stand out. Two years later, laying low was still engrained in her brain. As she approached the car and put her key in the lock, a big Ford truck, newer model, pulled up into the stall next to her car. Kinley looked at the big, red beast of a pick-up and, as the door swung open, the first thing she saw was a big bouquet of flowers emerging.

Reed climbed out of the car, smiling at her. "Hi," he said, holding the bouquet in one big hand. "I was hoping to catch you before you left."

Kinley still had the key in the door lock, looking over the top of her car at the man and feeling rather dumbfounded. But she was simultaneously aware of another feeling as she looked at him; she realized that she was glad to see him. Something about that Marlboro Man in the flesh made her heart skip a beat.

"Uh... hi," she said, her eyes twinkling rather humorously. "Nice flowers."

"Thanks."

"Got a date?"

He shrugged. "I was kind of hoping," he said. "I haven't exactly asked her out yet."

Kinley lifted her eyebrows. "Really?" she said, knowing instinctively that he meant her and torn between the excitement and apprehension of it. "Well, good luck."

He could see she was shutting the conversation down and he wasn't going to let her, not this time. She was good at warming him to a conversation and then fleeing, but it wasn't going to work tonight. He shut the door of the truck and began to move around her car.

"Do you think the flowers will do the trick?" he asked.

Kinley was very aware he was coming around the trunk of her car and into her personal space.

"Maybe," she said. "They're very nice."

"Hypothetically speaking, if a man brought you flowers like these, would you at least feel sorry for him enough to go get a cup of coffee with him?"

He was nearly upon her by this time, the big yellow and gold mums in between them. Gazing up into his handsome face, she was still torn between excitement and anxiety, but the excitement side was winning. Even as she tried to grasp at the invisible strands of diminishing apprehension, her excitement in a handsome man's interest overwhelmed her.

"Why are you asking me?" she asked. "You should be asking her."

"I am." He held the flowers up, smiling hopefully. "These are for you. I would be deeply honored if you'd accompany me someplace where we could have a cup of coffee."

He said it so sweetly. It was really a darling, little proposal. Kinley couldn't help the grin on her face, feeling herself relent. The apprehension was gone, edged out by the thrill. She reached out and reluctantly took the flowers when he held them out to her.

"Wow," she finally said, looking at the flowers. "That's the nicest offer I've had in a while. But I don't think...."

"Please," he cut her off. "Just let me buy a cup of coffee for the woman who saved my life."

She looked up at him, the smile gone from her face.

Then she swallowed hard, looking back at the flowers as indecision wracked her.

"You really don't have to do that," she said softly.

"I do," he insisted, his voice quiet. "Look, I'll be honest; what you don't get is that when we met two years ago at that greasy spoon out on the highway, within the first thirty seconds of knowing you, I had already decided I was going to ask you out. You were sweet and beautiful, and you just had this glow about you. Now, I don't get out much and I certainly don't go around saying this to every woman I meet, but when I saw you yesterday again, it was like... like the sun just burst out from behind the clouds. There you stood, like a dream or an angel, and you've been all I can think about ever since. I just... I suppose I just want to thank you for what you did and hopefully make a new friend in the process."

Kinley just stared at him. She was fully prepared to refuse him and run off, but she couldn't seem to muster the will. Truth be told, she wanted to get to know him, too. It wasn't healthy for her in the least, but he had managed to break down her resistance. After a moment, she simply nodded.

"Okay," she agreed softly. "You win. Where do you want to go?"

Reed smiled broadly. "There's a tearoom down the street that's open for dinner."

She nodded. "I know it," she said. "I'll meet you over there."

"Do you want to drive with me? It'll save your gas."

She had to chuckle. "I drive a Toyota," she pointed out, but surrendered when she saw his hopeful expression. "Oh, all right. But you're not a serial killer or anything, are you?"

"Only in the winter months."

"Good," she said, locking up her car. "Then I'm safe, at least for now."

Reed followed her around to the passenger side of his truck and opened the door for her. "You're safe in any case," he said, holding the flowers as she climbed in. Then he handed them back to her, his eyes fixed intently on hers. "You'll always be safe with me around, okay? I would never let anything happen to you."

God, what a chivalrous declaration. If he only knew. Kinley smiled weakly. "I believe you."

The smile faded from his face, replaced with a deadly serious expression. "I hope you do."

————

The Tea Room was a big competitor for the breakfast and lunch crowd against the Coffee Cakery, so much so that they had to open up at dinnertime just to make up for lost revenue. When the owner saw Kinley come in, she fell all over herself getting her the right table and making sure everything was perfect. When the blonde, overly-done owner provided them with two garishly-designed menus and left the table, Kinley wriggled her eyebrows.

"She's probably in the back figuring out how to poison my food," she teased softly.

Reed grinned as he looked at the menu. "Don't worry about it," he said. "I'll go back there and watch every move they make as they cook your food."

Kinley giggled. "Nothing intimidating about a big deputy hanging over their shoulder," she confirmed.

He looked up at her. "Me?" he said, feigning shock. "Intimidating?"

"Yes, *you*," she insisted, though it was with humor. "You're a very big man with a gun. Do you intend to break out your service weapon and wave it around back in the kitchens while they make my meal?"

He couldn't help but laugh at the mental image. Then he threw his hands up in the air and feigned waving a gun around for a couple of seconds as Kinley giggled uncontrollably. Because she was laughing, he was laughing. She had a gorgeous smile and a silly little giggle. He liked it a lot. The owner of the Tea Room came back to the table with two glasses of water in her hands as they were snorting and chuckling.

"You two are having a good time already," she said with too much enthusiasm. "What can I get you for dinner tonight?"

Kinley and Reed settled down, looking at each other and shrugging. "Uh," Kinley said, quickly looking over the menu. "I'm not sure what I'll have. What do you recommend?"

The bouffant-lady seriously considered the question. "We have a lovely endive and shrimp salad."

She had pronounced "endive" as "ahhhhhn-deev", which almost sent Kinley into giggles again. The woman was pretentious. "Great," she said, trying not to grin. "I'll take that."

The owner smiled thinly at her, perhaps sensing the fact that she was being laughed at, and turned to Reed. "And you, sir?"

Before he could open his mouth, Kinley interrupted. "Do you have anything with bacon?" she asked the owner.

Reed grinned broadly, shaking his head, as the owner nodded. "We have a chicken and bacon Florentine that's very delicious."

Reed handed her the menu. "I'll take it."

With a bob of the head to acknowledge the choices, the owner wandered away through the romantically-lit room. Reed was still smiling when Kinley picked up her water glass and returned her attention to him. She returned his smile, rather bashfully, and sipped her water.

Reed was careful in the manner in which he started the conversation. Knowing what he did since the research he had done earlier in the day, he was pretty sure what subjects to avoid. As skittish as she was, he didn't want to chase her off.

"So," he said, folding his big hands on the table in front of him. "What made a girl like you want to open up a restaurant?"

Kinley shrugged as she set her water glass down. "It's

something I always wanted to do," she said. "My grandmother was a wonderful cook and I learned from her."

"Where was she from?"

"Texas," she replied. "My parents were both born there. My grandmother could throw a little of this and a little of that into a pot and it would be the most delicious thing you've ever tasted."

"So you took the family talent public."

"I did."

"Did you go to culinary school?"

She nodded. "The Cordon Bleu in Pasadena, California. I went right out of high school when I really didn't know what I wanted to do yet with my life. My mom said I had to do something, so I picked culinary school because I thought it would be easy. Imagine my surprise when I found out it wasn't."

She made a face and he smiled. "I can only imagine," he said. "So your folks are from Texas. Where did you grow up?"

"Pasadena," she said, her smile fading.

"Do your parents still live there?"

Her smile vanished and she averted her gaze, He knew immediately that they had drifted onto one of those taboo subjects. He hastened to change the focus before she could answer.

"My grandfather on my mother's side is from England," he said. "He comes from a family with a family tree a mile long. When I was a kid, he used to tell me that I was descended from knights. He and I used to go in the back yard and fight each other with sticks, pretending they were swords. My mom used to get pissed about it. Well, pissed about that and the fact that Grandpa also taught me how to insult people in French."

She lifted her eyes from the tabletop, smiling wanly at his sense of humor. "What did he teach you?"

"Votre mère est un hamster."

She burst out laughing. "What does that mean?"

"Your mother is a hamster."

She continued to giggle. "Do you use it often?"

"Often enough," he said. "It also came in handy when I lived in Washington D.C. You'd be surprised how many times I needed to insult someone in French."

As he'd hoped, her attention was diverted from the taboo subject and she seemed to take interest in the conversation again. At least now she was grinning.

"I'd believe it," she said. "I would also believe that you've come from a long line of knights."

"Why's that?"

"Because you look like what I would imagine them to look like," she said. "You said yesterday that you worked for the Marines?"

He nodded. "Captain Reed D. McCoy until I opted out."

"Why did you opt out?"

His good humor faded somewhat. "It was time, I guess," he said. "Plus, my dad needed me here."

"What do you mean?"

He sat back in his chair, relaxing to the conversation.

"My dad is the sheriff of Fremont County," he said. "His office is based in Lander, south of Riverton, but his jurisdiction is all of Fremont County. We also work in conjunction with the Lander Police Department and the Shoshone Police Department. About three years ago, my dad became sheriff and cleaned house. Turned out there was some corruption going on and he got rid of the problem children. There's still a lot of stuff going on, but it's getting better. Or, at least, it's not out of control. We're getting a handle on it. He asked me if I'd be willing to come back and work for him, so I did."

Kinley listened with interest. "It must have been quite a change from the Marines."

"Not much," he said. "A cop is a cop. I was with the military police before I joined Investigative Services, so it really wasn't all that different."

She thought on that a moment, thinking back to her own career in the Los Angeles Sheriff's Department. But she wasn't willing or ready to speak of that yet. That was something that stayed locked up deep inside her. She sincerely wished she could have spoken with him about it because it seemed like they had a lot in common. So, she simply nodded.

"What about family?" she asked. "Did you have to uproot them from Washington to move them back here?"

He cast her a long glance. "You're assuming I'm married."

She cocked an eyebrow in return. "I'm assuming you're

not if you asked me out to dinner. If you are, then I'll be leaving."

He shook his head, putting his big hand on hers as they rested on top of the table. "I was," he said quietly. "That ended about eight years ago. When I came back to Wyoming, it was just me. My two boys live with their mother on the east coast and visit me during the summer. It was hard being away from them at first, but then I just got used to it. I really miss them sometimes."

Kinley was staring at him. *It was hard being away from them at first. I really miss them sometimes.* At least he got to see his children. She never would again. She didn't feel the least bit sorry for him; not one little bit, but in the same breath, she felt some sympathy. She understood what it was like to be separated from one's children. She understood all too well.

For an evening that had been going so beautifully well, she could feel the familiar grief and pain welling up in her chest. His innocent statement had her panic rising and it was becoming increasingly difficult to breathe. She knew she had to get out of there, away from him, before she exploded into a million slivers of anguish.

She tried hard not to think of her children; so very hard. She blocked them out, ignored the memories, because it was the only way she could retain her sanity. To pretend they never existed was the only way. But as Reed spoke quietly of his boys, she could suddenly see two little, smiling faces looking back at her, a girl of seven and a boy of six. They tried to speak to her but she shut her eyes, blocking them out again. Her panic had reached the boiling point. She had to get out of there.

"I... I need to use the restroom," she said, bolting to her feet and snatching her purse. "I'll... be right back."

Reed started to stand up but she was already gone, moving very quickly through the dining room and back into the hallway toward the rear where the restrooms were. Her head was down and her manner was edgy. He thought, perhaps, he should go with her to make sure she was okay, but he decided it was better not to. She might think he was being needy or clingy or, even worse, nosy. So he forced himself to sit back down and wait for her to return. He thought hard on their conversation, wondering what might have upset her so. She had such a habit of running away. Something in the woman was so deeply hurt and so deeply tragic.

Dinner was served a few minutes later. He really wasn't surprised when Kinley never came back.

FIVE

AT FOUR O'CLOCK THE next morning, Reed was waiting for her.

He was on-duty and supposed to be in Lander twenty-five miles away, but he had to see Kinley. The woman had run off last night in the midst of their dinner date and he was the cause of it. He had to apologize or, at the very least, make sure she was all right. By the time he'd figured out she had abandoned their conversation, her car was gone when he drove back over to the Coffee Cakery.

So he went home, got up at two-thirty in the morning, and logged in early for his shift before driving the twenty-five miles back to Riverton to wait for Kinley to show up to work. Even now, he and his unit were parked in the shadows of a big Poplar tree, watching the entire parking lot from where he sat. He watched as the employees began arriving for the early morning shift, busboys and cooks alike. He could see the lights going on in the restaurant as the place was readied for the coming day.

Eventually, a tan Toyota pulled into the lot and he recognized it as Kinley's car. Setting his coffee in the cup holder, he turned on his unit and pulled out from the shadows, shooting across the parking lot, and pulling up behind Kinley's car just as she was climbing out of it. He was effectively blocking her in. He would be smart about it this time if she tried to run.

Kinley put up her hand to shield her eyes from the headlights, having no idea who it was until Reed turned the car off and the headlights dimmed. As he climbed out of the car, a very big man in his khaki uniform, her hand came down and apprehension registered across her face.

Reed walked right up to her. He was concerned, edgy, and tired of playing games. He felt so much attraction to the woman that he couldn't verbalize it; all he knew was that he wanted her, and everything about her, and they were going to have it out at that moment. He spent all night building up a righteous rage filled with sorrow and regret and hope. He just couldn't keep quiet any longer.

"Are you okay?" he demanded.

Kinley nodded, stumbling back somewhat because he had planted himself right in front of her. "I'm fine," she said, apprehensive. "Look... I'm sorry I left last night. I want you to know that...."

He cut her off. He wasn't going to listen to her anymore. He was going to get it all out and let the cards fall where they may.

"You're going to hear what I have to say first," he said, his deep voice low and threatening. "I'm going to say this here and now so it's all out in the open. Kinley, I've already told you how attracted I am to you. I told you that I have felt that way since the moment I met you. The conversations we've had that end up with you running off or ditching me have been some of the most wonderful conversations I've ever had. I can see this beautiful personality beneath this mysterious façade you keep up. I see someone I want to get to know very well. Whatever I said last night to make you leave me sitting alone in a restaurant... I'm sorry. I'm so sorry. But, honey, you've been running from me since the first day I met you and I wanted to know why. Clover Fields wouldn't tell me anything. But Kinley Connors-Berrington did."

By this time, Kinley was pressed up against her car, appearing as if she were recoiling from him. Tears were welling in her eyes and her breathing quickened. She lowered her head and tried to move away from him.

"I have no idea what you're talking about," she claimed.

"Yes, you do."

She could tell, simply by the expression on his face, what he meant. She began to feel nauseous. All of it, the dark secrets and the horrific past, were about to come front and center. She wasn't ready for it.

"No," she breathed. "Please... no. For the love of God, don't..."

He grasped her by the wrists so she couldn't slip away.

"I want you to listen to me and listen carefully," he whispered urgently. "I know what happened in Los Angeles. I read all about it. You were a decorated officer for the Los Angeles Sheriff's Department until the brother of a criminal, scum bastard you put in jail came after you. I read that he ambushed your husband and two small children one morning on the way to school. I read that after their murders, you disappeared. People think you're dead, honey. Did you know that? The Los Angeles Sheriff's Department has listed you as missing and presumed dead."

By now, she was weeping softly, her head hung as he gripped her wrists. "Please," she sobbed, sinking to her buttocks against her car. "Please don't say anymore. Please..."

He shifted his grip so he had a better hold on her. Crouched down beside her, he held on to her tightly. "I'm so sorry, Kinley," he confessed. "I'm so sorry you had to go through that. I can't even imagine what you must have gone through. But are you in witness protection? Is that why you're hiding out here in Wyoming?"

She shook her head, so hard that her neat ponytail slapped around and pieces of hair came free. "It's none of your business," she said. "Please let me go. None of this is any of your business."

He didn't loosen his grip. "You're right," he said softly, steadily. "It's none of my business. If this was any other situation or anyone else, I wouldn't have bothered. But you... you saved my life. I have an emotional investment in you. I also think you're the most alluring and beautiful woman I've ever met and I just want to help."

That seemed to ease her somewhat, although she was still hanging her head, crying. "You can't help," she whispered. "This is my deal and nobody can help."

He sighed. "Will you at least tell me why the L.A. Sheriff's Department has you listed as missing?" he persisted quietly. "If you're in witness protection, please tell me so I can help you if the need arises. Will you please just tell me why you're here?"

Her head shot up and the green eyes flashed. "I'm here because I can't face it," she half-shouted. Now, it was all starting to come out. "Tom was driving *my* car that day; those gangbangers thought it was me and shot it full of holes. When they came to tell me what had happened to Tom and the kids, I got into Tom's car and just started driving. I drove and drove and drove until I came to the most desolate place I could find. I didn't have any clothes or money or anything. I left my cell phone back in Los Angeles. I drove until the road ended in Green River, Wyoming and then I just couldn't go on anymore. I ended up at the Hi-Way Café and sat there for seven hours until the owner figured out something was wrong. He ended up hiring me as a waitress because he felt sorry for me and paid me five hundred bucks for a seventy-hour work week. I lived in a tiny trailer with no air conditioning and a broken bathtub, but it was a blank slate without anything that reminded me of my husband and children. It was a place where I could pretend I had no past. Don't you get it? I can't face any of it. My family died because of *me*."

She hung her head again, tears returning with a vengeance. Sighing with great sadness, Reed put a big hand on her lowered head, stroking the soft, blonde hair. He felt as bad as he possibly could.

"So you're trying to start a new life up here," he said softly. A great many things were coming clear to him now. "Why did you run off after you shot those suspects at the Hi-Way Café? You weren't in any trouble."

She wiped at her face. "I ran off because I couldn't handle talking to the police or going through the report process," she said. "I knew my real identity would come out eventually. I wanted to be incognito, a nobody, and the thought of involving myself in something like that... I just couldn't handle it. Emotionally, I just couldn't do it. I had to keep running."

He continued to stroke her head, comfortingly. He still held one of her wrists and he lifted her hand, bringing it to his lips for a gentle kiss.

"You had to keep avoiding it," he whispered.

She nodded as the tears continued to pour. "I lost my whole family," she whispered. "That part of me is dead."

He kissed her hand again. "You just ran off and left your parents, your friends, your family... everything... behind?"

She covered her face with her hands. "I couldn't bury my kids," she wept. "God, I just couldn't do it. I couldn't deal with other people's grief. They would want to talk to me and hug me and... and remind me every second of the day of what I had lost. I just couldn't do it."

She was sobbing heavily by now and he sat down next to her on the asphalt, pulling her into his enormous embrace. He didn't know what else to do. He sat there, his face against the side of her head, feeling her heave with sobs. It was such a tender embrace, one of deep sympathy and comfort. He'd never known anything like it. In his own way, he understood her position completely.

"I think you and I have more in common than you realize," he commented. "When I was a senior in high school, I had a girlfriend I intended to marry. We had been together for three years and she was everything to me. After our senior prom, we went to a few parties and I made sure not to drink. I wanted to get her home safe, and me home safe, because we had our whole lives ahead of us. I was a responsible kid... I didn't drink or smoke. I was always trying to do the right thing. Anyway, it was about two in the morning and we were heading back from a party at my buddy's house. We were two blocks from her home when a drunk driver blew the stop sign and plowed into the passenger side of my car. The impact broke her neck and killed her immediately. When I went to Annapolis, in a sense, I was running like you are. I just couldn't handle it. I blamed myself. I never even came back here until three years ago, and that just brought the guilt back. I guess I never really dealt with it, so in a small way, I get where you are coming from. I really do."

By this time, Kinley's sobs had lessened. She gazed up

at him, wiping at her face, feeling a kindred spirit in him with his confession. More than that, she felt a huge amount of comfort in his warm embrace.

She hadn't been held by anybody in years. It was enough to melt her, console and soothe her, and she ended up laying her head against his chest. Although she could feel the Kevlar vest underneath, it was still a wholly marvelous sensation.

"I'm sorry," she finally said, her voice hoarse and faint. "It really sucks to lose someone you love. It's really a messed-up, screwed-up world sometimes."

"It sure is."

"Do you feel like you've been able to deal with her death since you've returned?"

He was careful in his reply. He didn't want to discourage her from finding her own healing path even if he was rather muddled about his.

"A little," he said, although it was a lie. "It becomes easier with time, I guess. I think all those years I had distanced myself from it, turned it into some big, impossible nightmare, more a creation of my mind than anything else. That made it really hard to face when I came back to Riverton."

She fell silent, locked in his arms, lying heavily against his chest. But at least she had stopped sobbing. He was grateful for small mercies.

"I still don't think I'm strong enough to face it," she finally said. "I don't want to."

"You will when you're ready."

"Maybe."

He was quiet a moment. "Can I ask you a question?"

"Yes."

"What were your kids' names?"

She sniffled before answering. "Violet and Liam," she said softly. "Vi was seven and Liam was six. Why do you ask?"

He hugged her gently. "Because I'll say a prayer for them," he said softly. "I'm a praying kind of guy."

She lifted her head and looked at him. "Thank you," she whispered sincerely. "That's really sweet."

He just smiled. Kinley was touched by his statement. In fact, she'd derived more comfort from the man than she'd ever known, from anyone, over the past three years. In some strange way, sitting with him on the asphalt as dawn broke over the Wyoming countryside had been therapeutic. At least she had been able to speak of her murdered family. That was a big step.

But it also left her emotionally drained and perhaps confused on a whole new level. As they sat against her car, a few more employees drove up and parked their cars. Not wanting to be seen in a passionate huddle with the deputy, Kinley gently pulled herself from his embrace and wearily stood up. Reed stood up beside her, helping her brush off her dark pants. Pale, her makeup smeared, she looked up into his handsome face.

"I think I'm going to go home for a while," she said. "I don't feel much like working this morning."

He met her gaze steadily. It was evident that he was

mulling something over. "I have a better idea," he said softly. "Why don't you take the day off and ride along with me? I'd love the company and we can talk some more if you want to. If you don't, that's okay, too."

Kinley shook her head. "I don't think so," she said, averting her gaze and brushing off her left knee. "I'm going to go home and... think about things. Or try not to think about them, as the case may be."

He was disappointed that she wouldn't come with him. He had truly hoped that somehow over the past couple of days, he had succeeded in breaking down her walls just a little. He very much wanted her to let him in. But he could see from the way she was looking at him that his knowledge of her situation, and the questions, might have done more harm than good. He'd shaken her up and that was never a good thing. There was a wariness in her eyes that hadn't been there before.

"Okay," he said softly. "Can I take you home?"

She wouldn't look at him. "No, thanks," she said. "I'll drive."

"Can I follow you to make sure you, at least, get home all right?"

She shook her head. "No," she said, starting to move back for her car and holding up a hand to him to prevent him from following. "Reed, please... you've made yourself very clear about everything. I'd be lying if I said I wasn't attracted to you as well, but you have to understand... I'm so broken right now. You're sweet and compassionate and attentive, but I just need to be left alone. I've spent all of this time being completely dependent on myself because it's just safer that way. There's no way to be hurt if you're only depending on yourself. I hope you understand that."

He hadn't felt so much disappointment in a very long time. "I'm sorry," he confessed. "I screwed up, didn't I? I didn't mean to invade your privacy. I just meant... well, I could tell there was something wrong. That's obvious. I just thought I could help if I knew what it was."

She shook her head, but kept the distance between them. "You didn't screw up," she said. "But this is something I have to face alone. Maybe... maybe you've helped me do that in some way. At least I'm thinking about my family now. I haven't let myself do that in a really long time. You've opened that door."

He didn't know what else to say. He felt like she was walking away from him forever and the distress was knifing him in the gut. "I'm never going to see you again, am I?"

Kinley looked at him. She could see the sorrow on his face and it struck a chord deep inside her. But the truth was that she couldn't answer his question; he wanted something more than she was able to give. Still, the thought of having the man in her life was a strong lure promising contentment and, perhaps, joy that she thought she'd lost. She really wasn't sure. Confusion was the only thing she could be certain of at the moment.

Impulsively, she went to him, throwing her arms around his neck and lifting her mouth to his. She caught Reed off guard with the power of her kiss, but he quickly recovered, his muscular arms going around her slender body as he held her against him. It was the most satisfying embrace of his entire life. Kinley kissed him sweetly, tenderly, and lustily. It was all things heaven rolled into one.

But as quickly as it started, she tried to end it. He felt her start to pull away but he wouldn't let her; he suckled her lower lip, snaking his tongue into her mouth and tasting her sweetness. He could feel her respond to him, her arms so tightly around his neck that she was binding the back of his skull, but then suddenly, she let him go. This time, he had no choice but to release her as she put her hands on his throat to push him away. Reed nearly fell over with the abrupt and rough action.

He called her name as she bolted into her car and slammed the door, locking it. Then she turned on the engine and turned on the radio so loud that he could hear it from the outside of the car. She couldn't go anywhere because his unit was pulled up behind her, so she sat there and buried her face in her hands, weeping painfully as he knocked on the window and tried to get her to look at him. She wouldn't do it.

Reluctantly, and still feeling that kiss zinging through every vein in his body, he got into his unit and prepared to back up, putting the truck into reverse and backing away so she could get out. But she didn't move, so he pulled out onto the boulevard. Then he parked down the street from the restaurant and turned off the lights, waiting for her to leave the parking lot. She did, eventually, and he fought off the urge to follow. He didn't think she'd take it very well.

Besides, he knew where to find her every morning of the week and he intended to do just that.

The next morning he was there when she pulled into the parking lot at four-thirty in the morning. He knew that she was aware of his presence; it was impossible not to be aware because of where he had parked his unit. But she wouldn't acknowledge him. Reed sat there and watched her go into the restaurant as if to make sure she made it to work okay before heading off to his day shift.

The same pattern went on for thirteen days like some sad and strange ritual, and on the days he wasn't working he would still show up and sit in his truck. Sadly, he would watch her enter her restaurant and that was the last he would see of her until the next day. But on the fourteenth morning, he woke up and realized he couldn't do it anymore. Emotionally, he had to forget about her because it was eating him up inside. She didn't want anything to do with him and he had to accept that.

He had to move on.

Driving to work that morning was a chore. More than a chore, he simply didn't want to go to work. As the sun rose in the east, turning the sky shades of pink and blue, he picked up his cell phone and dialed the number of his best friend. The man lived a thousand miles away and had for years, but that didn't matter. Beau Meade would be Reed's best friend until they were old and gray and in rockers. Even if the rockers weren't in the same nursing home, Beau and Reed would still be linked.

He just needed to hear a friendly voice.

Beau picked up on the third ring.

"What a coincidence," Beau said. "I talked to Trace a couple of days ago. Seems like this is homecoming week."

Reed smiled weakly. "Is that right?" he said. "How is Trace?"

"Building stuff," he said, referring to their other close friend, Trace Rocklin, who lived in California. "Trying to settle down into civilian life."

"Still?"

"Putting aside the Eliminator is going to take time."

"Is he okay?"

"He's good enough," Beau said. "He suggested we all meet in Reedville or Memphis and spend a weekend stuffing our faces with good barbeque. You in?"

"You know I am," Reed said. "When?"

"I'm not sure yet," Beau said. "We'll get Trace on a conference call one of these days and figure it out."

"Good," Reed said. "God knows, I could use it."

"Oh?" Beau said. "Why? What's going on with you?"

Reed paused. "Hell, I don't know," he said. "Frustration, mostly."

"Why?"

Reed sighed heavily. "You remember a few years ago when I almost bought it at a highway restaurant down in Fremont?" he said. "Three guys came in to rob the place and they were about to take me out when one of the waitresses saved my life?"

"I remember," Beau said, sobering dramatically. "I have

to tell you that when you told me the story... it scared the shit out of me, Reed."

"You remember the waitress we tried to find?"

"I think so. Why?"

"Because I found her."

"Seriously?" Beau said, sounding interested. "That's great news... isn't it?"

"It is," Reed said. "You know the only thing she left behind when she ran out of the Hi-Way Café was her purse, which really only contained a few dollars and her driver license. It was fake."

Beau, who was also in his unit and driving home from a graveyard shift, yawned. The man was the county sheriff of Tallahassee County in rural Mississippi, a post he'd assumed in the years since his CIA days. Because of his line of work, and Reed's, they often had a lot of business to talk about, so he well remembered the story behind Reed's mysterious savior.

"I think we figured it was, didn't we?" he said. "I seem to remember that. So what's her story? Where has she been?"

"In Riverton," Reed said simply. "I was born and raised there. My parents still live there. She owns the hot new restaurant in town."

"And you had no idea?"

"No," Reed said. "I don't go to Riverton much. Too many memories, so I just steer clear."

Beau thought on that. "Wow," he said. "So she was there all the time. Have you talked to her?"

"I have," Reed said. "At first, she was freaked out to see me, but she's calmed down since then, but not a lot. Only enough for us to have a few conversations and I tried to take her out to dinner once, but she skipped out on me."

On the other end of the line, Beau sighed. "Well," he said after a moment. "Sounds like she's got some issues."

"That's an understatement," Reed said. "Not to go into a ton of detail, but I did a little investigating once I knew her real name. She's ex-LAPD, a decorated officer, and she was the victim of a gang attack. Killed her whole family."

"Oh, Jesus," Beau said with sorrow. "That's rough."

"No joke."

"But what's she doing in Wyoming?"

"Running," Reed said simply. "Running from what happened, running from life. She's just... running."

"Poor lady," Beau said. "But at least you found her. Did you thank her for what she did for you during that robbery?"

"Repeatedly," Reed said. "I even took her out to dinner to thank her. Hell... that's not exactly true. She does something to me, Beau. When I look at her, I feel something."

"That's because she saved your life."

"I felt it before that. The first time I looked at her, I felt something."

Beau didn't say anything for a moment. "Look, Reed," he said seriously. "You know I wouldn't tell you how to live your life, but I don't think this woman sounds like she's relationship material. Sounds like she's got a lot of demons she needs to get control of before you need to get involved with her. Otherwise, she's going to pull you down with her and you really don't need that."

"I know," Reed said sadly. "I know better than anyone that you can't fix someone, but that hasn't stopped me from trying."

"And?"

"And she shut me down pretty hard."

"Good," Beau said. "She knows she's not good for you, so do yourself a favor and just stay away from her for now. If it's meant to be... she'll come to you."

"I suppose."

"Seriously, Reed. You can't force something like this."

Reed knew that. He could see the sheriff's station up ahead, signaling the start of another day. Another day just like any other day, only this time, he would be considerably more depressed.

But he'd just have to get over it.

"You're right," he said. "Hey, I'm at work, so I'll let you go. Next time you can tell me how things are in your neck of the woods. And we can talk about that barbeque weekend."

"Sounds good," Beau said. "And just so you know, things are going well in my neck of the woods."

"Really?" Reed said as he turned into the parking lot. "What's going on?"

"A conversation for another time," Beau said. "But let's just say you're not the only one who has met someone."

"Seriously?" Reed said, hitting his brakes a little too hard because he was surprised. "You've got a girlfriend?"

"Maybe," Beau said mysteriously. "Like I said – a conversation for another time. There honestly isn't much to tell right now, so I'm not being evasive, but maybe I'll have more to tell you next time."

"Excellent," Reed said. "I'm looking forward to it."

"Take care, my friend."

"You, too."

Putting the car in park and turning off the engine, Reed felt a little better. Talking to his old friends always did that to him. Time talking to Beau, and to Trace, was always time well spent. It solidified the fact that he wasn't all alone in life.

He still had his friends.

And always would.

Opening the car door, he was ready to face the day.

SIX

HEADING into the small sheriff's station in Lander, Reed started his shift at six in the morning. When he entered the one-storied brick building, constructed in the middle of the last century, he could already hear the chatter on the police band from dispatch and he could smell the coffee. The morning was busy at this early hour. Just as he passed by the break room and headed to the bank of mailboxes, one of the clerks stuck her head out.

"Reed," she said. "There's someone here to see you."

He looked over his shoulder at her as he pulled his mail out of his mailbox. "Okay," he said. "What's it about?"

"I don't know," the clerk said. "She wouldn't say."

"Name?"

"Wouldn't tell me that, either."

He was still rifling through his mail. "Did you check her for weapons?"

It was a sarcastic question. The dispatcher smirked. "Nope," she said. "That's your job."

He just lifted an eyebrow. "Where is she?"

"Briefing room."

His eyes were glued to his mail as he made his way down the hallway toward the briefing room, which was little more than a large office. Entering through the door, he caught a glimpse of a body seated in a chair to his right and he lifted his gaze to focus on the woman. When he did, the mail tumbled right out of his hand.

He knew the face very well.

"Hi," Kinley said as she smiled timidly.

Reed was astonished. Thrilled, but astonished. "Hi," he said, reaching down to clumsily pick up his mail in scattered pieces. "What are you doing here? Is everything okay?"

Kinley stood up and helped him pick up his fallen mail. She handed him a couple of pieces from where they had slipped under her chair.

"Everything's fine," she said quietly, eyeing the open door as he set his mail down. "Can we, uh, shut the door?"

He was nodding before she even got the sentence out of her mouth, shutting the briefing room door and then facing her expectantly. He was rattled by her appearance and struggling not to be. He didn't want to scare her off again but he had a lot of thoughts and emotions bubbling in his chest at the moment.

"I never thought I was going to see you again," he said honestly. "How did you know where to find me?"

Kinley watched him take the seat next to her. He looked so incredibly nervous. Truth was, she was nervous, too.

"You said you weren't stationed in Riverton," she said. "This is the headquarters for the sheriff so I used my police training and my great deductive reasoning and figured you must be here."

Reed was having difficulty doing anything other than just staring at her. "Good job," he said. He started to say something but thought better of it and shut his mouth. After a moment, he simply shook his head. "I'm really scared right now that I'm going to say something that is going to send you running again. I don't want to screw this up."

Kinley gave him a crooked smile. "Then why don't you let me do the talking?"

"Happy to."

Kinley gazed into his eyes, her smile fading. *Where to start?* She chuckled nervously and looked at her hands.

"I had it all planned out what I was going to say to you and now that I'm here, I'm at a loss," she said, fiddling with her fingers. "I guess... I guess what I want to say most to you is that I'm sorry. You've gone out of your way to be kind and concerned, and I've acted like an idiot. I want you to know that up until three years ago, I was the most stable person you'd ever want to meet. I was the valedictorian of my high school, I graduated college with honors, and I had the same boyfriend since my sophomore year in high school who was the guy I ended up marrying. I'm not a game player and I don't jerk people around. I know right from wrong and I have a good moral compass. I'm just so sorry that your acquaintance with me hasn't conveyed that. I'm sorry if I hurt your feelings or embarrassed you."

He shook his head. "You haven't done either of those things," he said. "I'm just sorry that I've been so clumsy in my attempts to get to know you. You made it clear you weren't interested. I should have listened."

She shook her head. "You're reading me all wrong," she said. "I *am* interested. That's the problem. I'm just not sure... emotionally, it scares me to death to open myself up to someone again."

"I completely understand."

She looked at her hands again, growing increasingly fidgety. "I don't have any friends here," she said quietly. "I don't have any friends, period. When I ran from L.A., I ran from everybody – my family, my friends – everybody. I just shut down and shut off. There were many times when I contemplated driving my car off a bridge or into a wall. I admit that I still have thoughts like that. But I know it wouldn't solve the problem. When I close my eyes at night, I still see my kids and wonder what they would have been like now, what interests they would have had. Vi was such an artist; she loved to draw. I wonder if she would have kept it up. Liam loved wild animals – lions, tigers, monkeys. He said he wanted to work in a zoo. I wonder if he would have. Anyway, what I wanted to say is this – over the past two weeks, you have shown up every morning when I arrived to work. I knew you were there. It gave me comfort even though I didn't want to admit it. Now that you're not doing it anymore, I miss it, and I realize how awful I've treated you. I... I just wanted to say I'm sorry."

He was listening carefully. "You didn't need to apologize," he said quietly. "But something has occurred to me."

She looked up at him. "What?"

"You've been running from everything and everyone, not just me. I'm just one in a long line of people and situations you've run from."

She sighed heavily and lowered her gaze again. "That's true."

"When are you going to stop running?"

She looked at him. "I'm not sure," she said. "I don't have a reason to."

"I'd like to give you a reason."

"What do you mean?"

"I mean that I want to be that reason."

Kinley stared at him. Then, she took in a long, deep breath. "You know," she said slowly, "my first instinct when you said that was to run off. Notice I didn't give in to it."

He grinned. "I'm glad. That's progress."

She reluctantly returned his smile, alternately looking at him and looking at her hands. She couldn't seem to maintain eye contact with him more than a few seconds at a time. Then, she reached out and grasped his big hand. He held her hand tightly between his two big ones, squeezing it. He was so thrilled that he could hardly control himself. She was here, she was sorry... and she was holding his hand.

"Thank you," she whispered, still staring at the ground. "For your patience and your gentleness around a woman who's kind of a freak."

He laughed softly, lifting her hand to kiss it. "She's not a freak," he insisted softly. "I think she's pretty wonderful. In fact... are you heading to work right now?"

Kinley nodded. "I am."

"Do you ever take a day off?"

She shook her head. "Never. I work seven days a week."

He tugged on her hand to get her to look up at him. When their eyes met, he lifted his eyebrows at her.

"Take today off," he demanded. "Call in sick. I want you to ride along with me. I'd like to spend time with you."

It was such a sweet offer. She gave him a rather lopsided grin. "In a patrol unit?"

He grinned in return. "You just never know what could happen," he shrugged, watching her giggle. "We could find some banditos or outlaws or run into a Shoshone war party. We might even run into that guy who dances with coyotes."

Her laughter grew. "I think it was dances with wolves."

He just watched her, finding her laughter so incredibly enchanting. "Coyotes, wolves... whatever," he said, sobering as he gazed into her eyes. "Come with me, Kinley. Please."

Her smile faded as she gazed into his eyes. It was

evident that she was weighing the request. Finally, she dipped her head in surrender.

"All right," she said softly. "I'll do it."

———

The sun was already up by the time they pulled out of the parking lot, heading south to Main Street. Kinley had made a call to the Cakery and told the day shift manager that she wasn't feeling well, clearing the way for a day to play hooky. The city was just coming alive, with people out walking their dogs and school buses throwing clouds of exhaust into the air.

It was nice, normal, and relatively quiet, but for Kinley, it was also relatively strange. It was the first time she had been in a patrol unit since the day before she'd lost her family. Her natural instinct was to bottle up the anxiety she was feeling to the point of panic but she thought perhaps that wasn't the best way to handle it. Reed had offered his shoulder, and everything else, to cry on. Maybe now was the time to begin building some trust between them.

She'd come this far... it was time for her to start opening up.

"Uh," she muttered, taking a deep breath. "I have to tell you that I'm feeling kind of uncomfortable right now."

Reed looked over at her. "Why?" he asked. "What's wrong?"

Kinley shifted in the seat and cleared her throat in a

nervous gesture. "Because I haven't been in a unit since everything happened," she said quietly. "The moment I got in, I wanted to get right back out again and run. Just the smell, the sights, the sounds... it's taking a lot of effort not to open the door and jump out."

He immediately pulled the car over to the curb. "If you're not comfortable, I'm not going to force you," he said seriously. "I'll take you back to the station."

He was being genuine and sincere about it. Kinley resisted the urge to agree. She grabbed his hand tightly and turned away, looking out the window.

"No," she said softly. "I have to face my fears sooner or later. Just... talk to me, would you? Keep my mind occupied so I don't go back to that day."

Reed held her hand snuggly as he put the car in gear and pulled away from the curb. "You got it," he said softly. "But before I start rattling away, tell me what subjects are off limits so you don't end up jumping out of the window."

Kinley grinned but even as she did so, her eyes began to fill with tears. She could feel them coming on, her eyeballs burning, and a lump formed in her throat. In spite of her resolve, she could feel a breakdown coming. She squeezed Reed's hand tightly.

"Oh, God," she breathed. "Maybe... maybe this isn't such a good idea. I haven't dealt with any of these feelings since the day it happened and right now, the smell of this car and the sound of the radio... everything... is bringing it back on me like it's all fresh and new and raw. Can you... can you please stop the car?"

Reed pulled over in a flash. They were in a mostly residential area and the second the car pulled close to the curb, Kinley let go of his hand and jumped out of the car. Reed threw the car into park and jumped out on the other side, running around the side of the car and grabbing her before she could get away. She fell against him, sobbing deeply, and her knees collapsed. He ended up practically carrying her.

"It's okay," he said soothingly, steadily. "I'll take you back to the station. Everything's going to be okay."

Kinley wept pitifully. "Oh, my God," she gasped. "I miss my babies. Why did that have to happen? Why did it have to be them?"

She was on a roll. Reed picked her up and carried her back to the unit, putting her into the front passenger seat and slamming the door, making it around to the driver's side just as she was opening her door and struggling to climb out again. He threw himself into the driver's seat, reached over, and slammed her door shut. Then he shut his own door and hit the master lock so she couldn't open any of them.

Kinley really didn't seem to notice much or even care that he had effectively trapped her. She had quickly descended into the world of misery, the one she had kept herself so carefully guarded against, but the experience of being in the police cruiser had been too much. The dam had burst and there was no way to stop it.

Reed took off in the direction of Main Street. In fact, he lit up the rotators and ripped through town westbound, blowing lights until he reached a street that headed south out of the end of town. As Kinley sobbed into her hands, he hit speeds in excess of one hundred miles an hour heading south into the wide-open high plains of Wyoming. He made short work of the southbound road until he came to Squaw Creek Drive. Hanging a right and nearly spinning out, he tore down Squaw Creek and into the red plateaus and scrub brush of the desolate countryside.

The road had intermittent houses on it, big and fairly wealthy spreads on several acres on an exclusive road. Reed finally turned off the rotators when he came to a dirt driveway that veered off the road to the north. He hit the gravel and tore up the dirt road, throwing up rooster tails of dust behind him. Up a hill and down into a wash he went, heading into what seemed to be a no man's land of rocks and hills and badlands. After about a quarter of a mile on the road, he ended up at a big gate attached to a massive fence that stretched out as far as the eye could see.

Reed hit a remote in his glove box and the gate rolled open. Kinley's hysterics had quieted but she was still weeping softly, worn out and exhausted. Reed passed her a concerned glance as the gate rolled open enough that he could get through it. Once through, he hit the remote again and the gate began to close. A half mile down from the gate along that gravel road, hidden among the plateaus and rocky hills, an entirely new world opened up.

It was green here because a decent sized creek ran through the property, feeding the dry soil and producing grass and other foliage. There were corrals here and two big barns, with horses in one and cattle in the other. There was even a chicken coop, although there were chickens both inside the fence and outside of it, scattered about. The entire scene was rather bucolic. At the end of the gravel road on the top of one of the plateaus stood a typical ranch house, two stories, with a long porch that ran the entire length of the front of the house. It was the crowning glory of the unique, little world it supervised out in the middle of the Wyoming plains.

Dogs ran out of the barn as Reed pulled the unit up to the house. He turned off the car and climbed out as four very happy, and very big, dogs wagged their tails and pawed eagerly at him. Usually he would pet and play with the dogs – two German Shepherds, a Rottweiler, and a giant Alaskan Malamute – but at the moment, he was too preoccupied to acknowledge them. He raced around the back of the unit and came to the passenger door.

Opening the door, he pulled Kinley out and picked her up again. She was utterly exhausted and not inclined to fight him about anything at this point, so she wrapped her arms around his neck and buried her face against his shoulder as he carried her up to the house. Keys in hand, he deftly opened the lock and shut off the alarm.

With the dogs following, he took Kinley back to the master bedroom, realizing he hadn't even made his bed that morning but hardly caring. He lay Kinley down on the messy sheets, eyeing her as she lay there with her eyes closed and makeup down her cheeks, before heading into the big bathroom and throwing open the medicine cabinet. He was back at her side in less than a minute with a pill in one hand and a glass of water in the other.

"Here," he whispered, pulling her up into a seated position. "Take this. It'll make you sleep."

Kinley was lucid but she was so overwrought with emotion that it made it difficult to think clearly. She caught a glimpse of the pill before he popped it into her mouth.

"What...?" she sputtered, mouth full.

"Shhhh," he murmured, holding the water to her lips. "Just drink."

She frowned and tried to push the water away. "What is it?" she demanded weakly. "You're not giving me something to knock me out so you can take advantage of me, are you?"

He cocked a droll eyebrow. "In your dreams," he teased softly. "Just take it. You need to take a nap for a few hours. Swallow it."

He practically poured the water into her mouth, forcing Kinley to swallow the pill he had put there. She gulped it down, still frowning, as he pushed her back down onto the bed. She was about to let him know that she wasn't pleased he was making her pop pills when the picture of two small boys on the nightstand caught her attention. Immediately, her demeanor changed. She grew serious.

"Are those your sons?" she asked.

Reed set the empty water glass down beside the bed. "Yes."

Kinley stared at them for several long moments. "How old are they?"

He sighed faintly as he began to peel off his duty jacket. "Christopher is ten and Jackson is eight."

Kinley gazed at the two handsome young men. "When was Christopher born?"

"June the fourth, two thousand and four."

Kinley continued to stare at the picture a moment. Then, her face crumpled and the sobs came again. "Violet was born on June the twentieth of that year," she wept. "She would have been ten years old this month."

The tears were back with a vengeance and Reed felt as bad as he possibly could. Slinging his jacket across the nearest chair, he sat down on the bed beside her and gently rubbed her back, trying to give her some comfort. Kinley had her hands over her face.

"I'm so sorry about this," she cried. "I was totally fine when I came to see you this morning but getting into the unit... it just triggered something. I'm so embarrassed."

He stroked her back. "No need," he assured her quietly. "From what you've said, you haven't really dealt with the situation, so... so maybe it's time. Maybe you just need to get it all out."

She didn't really say much to that. She continued to keep her face covered as she sobbed. "Do you know why I wasn't driving my car that morning?" she asked. "I was pregnant and had really bad morning sickness, so Tom took the kids instead. He used my car because it was the last one in the driveway and blocking his car in. That goddamn gangbanger was waiting for my car when it passed through a major intersection by our house and he and his buddies pulled up on both sides of it and opened fire. Tom was killed instantly when a bullet hit him in the head and crashed the car into a light pole. Witnesses said that then the cars pulled up behind the crashed car, walked up, and emptied out two or three clips into the car, killing the kids. They never had a chance."

Reed closed his eyes tightly to ward off the horror of what she was telling him. He felt so sick for her. He lay his head down on her shoulder, his hand still on her back, trying to give her what meager comfort he could.

"I'm so sorry, honey," he whispered. "I can't even imagine what you went through. I'm so very sorry."

Kinley was so exhausted from weeping that the tears were starting to taper off as she recalled that very dark day with great clarity. She could see every moment that passed, feeling every emotion as if just feeling it for the first time. The grief was agonizing but, very quickly, it became numbing as her mind switched into self-protection mode. It was either that or she would surely lose her sanity. She began to take on an oddly glazed look.

"I was feeling so bad from the morning sickness that I had fallen back asleep once Tom and the kids left the house," she continued. "The next thing I realize, someone is pounding at my door. When I got up, I saw four units outside my house. I really had no idea that anything was wrong, at least not with Tom and the kids, until the lieutenant began to talk. He had to tell me the story three times before it sank in and I could actually comprehend what had happened. After that... I really don't remember much about the rest of the day other than getting into Tom's car that night and driving off. And I just kept driving."

Reed rubbed her back, kissing her shoulder before pushing himself up. "Kinley, don't think you have to talk about this," he said softly. "If you just want to go to sleep for a while, I'll sit here with you so you won't be alone."

She turned her head to look up at him, her face with its haunting beauty, etched with grief. "You're probably wondering what happened to the pregnancy."

He shook his head. "Not really. I suppose it doesn't matter in the long run."

She sighed and looked away, her lids growing heavy as the emotions rolled over her. "I was only a few weeks along," she whispered. "I guess the emotional upheaval and the fact that I didn't eat or take care of myself for weeks took its toll; I miscarried the day I ended up at the Hi-Way Café. I flushed the baby down the toilet in the restaurant. That's why I sat there for so long. I was trying to work up the courage to drive the car into an overpass because I literally had nothing left to live for. My entire family was dead."

Reed's gaze lingered on her for a moment before standing up. He removed his Sam Browne belt and laid it carefully on the chair, followed by his uniform shirt. He had a t-shirt underneath, sexy as hell as it strained against his broad chest. Then he took the radio out of the holster on the duty belt and told Dispatch that he was indisposed for the next hour. When they pressed him, he shut them down and turned the radio off. Then, he carefully crawled onto the bed and got in behind Kinley as she lay there sniffling.

"Can I just lay here and hold you for a few minutes?" he whispered. "It would make me feel a lot better."

Exhausted, and now being swept up in whatever drug he had given her, Kinley managed a weary grin. "It would make *you* feel better?"

"Yes," he said. "I'm feeling really sad right now and it's been years since I've held a woman I really wanted to hold. Would it be okay?"

Kinley couldn't even think about the fact that she was lying in the man's bed and he had given her a drug of unknown origin. It had been very stupid, in hindsight, but on the other hand, she didn't much care. She knew he wouldn't hurt her and, after what she had just experienced, she realized she needed the comfort of human contact. She needed Reed.

"Sure," she whispered.

Big, muscular, and warm arms went around her and Kinley sank back against him, feeling his heated body come into contact with hers. It was wildly arousing and wildly comforting. All of her restraint left her and she gave in to his heat, gripping his hands and pulling his arms more tightly around her, relishing in the feel of his touch. She was all wrapped up in him, and he in her, as she finally drifted off into a heavy, dreamless sleep.

It was the best rest she'd had in three years.

SEVEN

WHEN KINLEY OPENED her eyes again, it was to a dark room. For a moment, she had no idea where she was but eventually, she remembered the events that had brought her to this moment in time. Very clearly, she remembered falling asleep in Reed's arms and it took her no time at all to realize that he was gone. Without his massive presence enveloping her, she felt very alone. She turned slightly, looking at the rest of the giant, king-sized bed, seeing that it was vacant but for her.

The bedroom door was closed but she could see light emitting from the other side. She could also hear pots and pans banging around and she was sure she could smell something cooking. Struggling out of bed, as she found that she was still quite groggy, she staggered to the bedroom door and opened it.

Four very big dogs were laying right outside of the door, their heads shooting up when the door opened.

Kinley liked dogs so she wasn't afraid of them but the truth was she was a bit disoriented and still very tired, so she carefully moved around the dogs, straining to catch a glimpse of the source of the light. As soon as she stepped out of the room, she was in a corridor of sorts and could see that the front door wasn't far off to her right. Directly in front of her was a darkened staircase that led up to the second floor and to her left was a rather wide-open kitchen.

There was a lot happening in the kitchen. As soon as he heard the bedroom door open, Reed swung around to see Kinley looking lost and weary. He set the plate in his hand down onto the counter and quickly went to her.

"Hey, Sleeping Beauty," he said softly. "How are you feeling?"

Kinley tried not to yawn in his face. She ended up wiping at her eyes, looking at her fingers and seeing the smeared mascara. "I'm not sure," she said. "What in the hell did you give me?"

"A Tylenol sleeping pill," he said. "Those things always help me. Besides, it was the strongest thing I had in the house. I thought it might help you calm down."

She wriggled her eyebrows, unable to stop the big yawn this time. "No wonder I feel like I've been hit by a truck," she said. She stopped looking around at her surroundings long enough to see that he was looking some-what anxiously at her. She couldn't help the embarrass-ment. "I'm okay. I don't even know what to say about imploding like that other than I'm really sorry. You must seriously think I'm a complete head case."

He grinned. "Like I said, you've been through a lot," he said. "I can't say that in similar circumstances that I would be even half as pulled-together as you are. In spite of what you think about your behavior, I think the total opposite. I see a woman who has suffered through the worst possible situation but she's survived. More than that, she's thriving. I think that's incredibly admirable, Kinley. You're so much stronger than you give yourself credit for."

Kinley wasn't so sleepy anymore as she listened to him. The light of warmth went on in her sleepy eyes. "That's one of the nicest things anyone has ever said to me," she said softly. "I'm glad you see that part of me because I sure don't."

He gave her a wink, a gesture of confidence and sex appeal that gave Kinley that familiar giddy feeling she was coming to associate with him.

"Come on," he said quietly, reaching out to take her hand. "I thought I'd cook for the restaurant owner, so don't laugh. I'm not much of a cook but I try. I thought you might be hungry."

Kinley was deeply touched by his gesture as he led her over to the big kitchen that was bright with canned lighting and smelling of garlic. She let him hold her hand. In fact, she held on to him tightly.

"Wow," she said as she saw the plates and garlic bread and pasta on the counter. "This looks great. What time is it, anyway?"

Reed didn't want to particularly let go of her hand but he couldn't hold on to her and serve her at the same time, so reluctantly he let her go and pulled out a chair for her at the breakfast bar.

"Almost seven," he said. "You slept about twelve hours."

Kinley took the seat, sighing heavily when she realized that it was well into the evening. "And you were here the whole time?"

He nodded as he went over to the stove and started dishing out pasta and sauce. "I called work and took the day off," he said. "You were exhausted and I wasn't about to leave you here alone."

Kinley looked at him seriously. Her eyes fluctuated, as if there were a million thoughts rolling through her head. It was evident she was pondering his statement, the situation in general.

"You know," she said after a moment, "I keep thinking that you're just too good to be true. What guy takes off work to babysit a basket case?"

He snorted. "Me."

"You don't have anything better to do?"

He lifted his eyebrows as he brought two plates of spaghetti over to the breakfast bar and put one in front of her. "I've got a lot to do," he said. "But I've got you just where I want you and I'm not going to let you out of my sight. How's that for an answer?"

Kinley giggled. "Are you *sure* you're not a serial killer or anything?"

"I told you, only in the wintertime."

She laughed as she inspected the dish in front of her. "I

guess I'm still safe for a little while," she said, picking up her fork. "This looks really good. You did this all yourself?"

He took a bottle of red wine off the counter and brought two glasses over. "I did," he said. "I used to cook for my boys all of the time, to tell you the truth. My ex-wife was not the cooking type."

Kinley was already digging into the spaghetti, which turned out to be delicious. "This is really good," she said, mouth full. "You did a good job."

He poured her a big glass of wine and then one for himself. "Thanks," he said. "It's actually my mother's recipe. Don't steal it for the restaurant, okay? If she gets wind of it, she'll beat me within an inch of my life."

Kinley giggled as she swallowed her bite and took the wine glass in her hand. "I swear, I won't steal it," she said. "We don't serve spaghetti, anyway, but if we did, all bets would be off."

He held out his glass to her, their eyes meeting over the plates of spaghetti. There was a warmth in her eyes that hadn't been there before as he clinked his glass against hers.

"To the future," he said softly.

For the first time in three years, she felt some confidence at that statement. "To the future," she agreed.

Reed took a sip of wine, watching her intently as she sipped at hers and set the glass down to reclaim her fork. She dug in with gusto, shoveling down the spaghetti as he began to eat.

"Now that I know the serious things about you," he

began, rolling spaghetti with his fork, "I want to find out the not-so-serious things. Like, what's your favorite color?"

Kinley laughed softly, covering her mouth with a napkin to mask the fact that her mouth was open. "Quid pro quo, deputy," she said. "If I tell you something, you have to tell me something."

He smiled because she was. "Fair enough. But I asked you first."

"Purple. How'd you get so many dogs?"

"Because I'm a sucker for big dogs and I can't say no when someone offers me a big breed puppy. How tall are you?"

"Five feet and five inches. How tall are *you*?"

"Six feet four and a half inches. What kind of movies do you like?"

"Old war movies or anything black and white. How long have you lived at this house?"

"My family has had this land for almost two hundred years and a house has stood here for almost that long. I bought the property from my parents. Are you an only child?"

"No, I have a brother. Are you?"

"I have two younger brothers, both in the military. How'd you get your name?"

"Because it was my grandmother's name. Do you always interrogate women like this on the second date?"

"Not unless I'm wildly attracted to them. Are you going to want to go home tonight after dinner?"

She stopped in the rapid-fire exchange, fighting off a

grin. "Are you going to give me another sleeping pill to knock me out if I say yes?"

"No. I was just asking."

"I'm guessing you're asking with a reason in mind."

He was pretending to be serious. "No reason, ma'am. I'm not trying to keep you here for improper reasons. I just don't want you to be alone if you're going to go home and have another meltdown."

Her smile faded and she sighed, looking back to her spaghetti. She began to twirl it with less enthusiasm than before. "I won't have another meltdown," she said softly. "Oddly enough, what happened earlier... well, as I sit here and think about it, I think it helped a lot. I still feel sad and devastated but... but I feel better, too. I think you had a lot to do with that. You were very comforting."

He watched her take a bite. "I hope so. I tried to be."

She nodded, chewing before swallowing. "I guess I just needed to let it all out and when you said that I had survived such a terrible thing and even thrived... I guess I have in a sense. But I had to change who I am in order to do it."

"What do you mean?"

She collected her glass of wine and sipped at it. "I mean that I had to totally erase any past," she said quietly. "Now, I'm a business owner, a single woman, living in a state I'd never even visited until that day I ended up at the Hi-Way Café. Kinley Connors-Berrington doesn't really exist anymore as she was. Now, she's someone completely different."

He thought on that a moment and picked up his wine glass as well, taking a big swallow. "Actually, I was wondering about that."

"About what?"

He looked at her. "In order to open that restaurant, you had to have some money. You also had to have a credit application and some kind of bank loan, I'm guessing. You said you left everything behind... how did you manage to open that restaurant with nothing?"

She smiled. "That's a fair question," she said. "Actually, I had some money from working at the café but it wasn't nearly enough to open a restaurant, so as for the cakery... I wasn't entirely truthful about not having had contact with my family. I have. My brother, in fact. He's the only one who knows where I am and what I'm doing. He's the one who took out the bank loan for me and he's technically the owner of the Coffee Cakery. But he's keeping my secret. My parents don't know anything and neither do my friends or my work. I told my brother if he told anyone about me that I really would disappear and he'd never hear from me again, so fear has kept him quiet. He understands my feelings and why I did what I did. He gets me. In fact, he bought me the house I have in Riverton."

He understood a great deal now. It made sense. "I don't blame you for asking your brother for help," he said. "He must be quite a guy to help you like this."

"He is. I adore him." She finished her wine and set her glass down, turning to him. "Now that you know my dark and dirty secret, fair is fair. Do you have anything dark and dirty to tell me?"

He thought a moment as he drank his wine. Did he? There were his years at the CIA that popped to mind, the dirty ops he'd done, the state secrets he'd kept. But that wasn't something she needed to know on the second date. She was revealing her own secrets, but he was going to keep his for a while.

"Not really," he said after a moment. "You know all about Heather and her death, and my ex and my kids. I guess I'm just not all that exciting."

She laughed softly. "You're nice and normal," she said, her eyes twinkling. "That's a very attractive quality."

He looked at her hopefully. "Really?"

"Really."

He just grinned, now looking rather bashful as he drained the last of his wine. "Is it an attractive enough quality that you might let me take you out on a real date?"

"Of course."

"How about tomorrow?"

She nodded. "That would be great."

Reed was feeling just about as hopeful and thrilled as he had in a very long time. Finally, he felt as if they were making progress. She was trusting him and he was joyful and relieved.

"I am very happy to hear that," he said, noticing that she was finished with her food. "Do you want some more?"

Kinley shook her head and picked up her plate purely out of habit, moving to put it in the sink. "No, thanks," she said as she turned the water on. "It was really great. Thank you so much."

"I'll do that," he said, trying to gently push her out of the way to take over the dish cleaning duty. "You go sit down and have another glass of wine. Just relax."

She graciously bowed away. "If I didn't do this for a living seven days a week, I might give you an argument about it. As it is, I'll just do what you tell me."

He smiled at her as he began to rinse off the plates and she moved back to the breakfast bar and the bottle of wine. Pouring herself another glass, she propped her butt on the stool to watch Reed do dishes. More than that, she was now afforded an unobstructed view of his backside and she liked very much what she saw. The man had an amazing form.

"Uh…" she said, eyeing his fabulous buttocks and thinking the first lustful thoughts she'd had in years. "So tell me about this house. It's been here for almost two hundred years?"

She'd asked the question just to get her mind off his ass but Reed was oblivious to her passionate thoughts. "Parts of the house have been," he said, opening up the dishwasher. "I'll show you around in a minute."

"How long have you lived here?"

He put the dishes in and shut the dishwasher door. Pulling off a paper towel, he dried his hands. "Since I moved back from D.C.," he said. "I was actually born in this house, but my parents moved to Riverton right about the time I entered school."

Kinley looked around her general area, surprise on her features. "You were *born* in this house?"

Reed gave her a lopsided grin. "Literally," he said. "Every generation of my family going back for two hundred years was born in this house. Actually, I was supposed to be the first hospital birth in the family but my mom went into labor so fast that there wasn't time. I was born right in that room you were sleeping in."

Kinley laughed softly. "Conceived and born in the same bed," she said. "That doesn't happen much anymore, I would think."

"No, it doesn't."

Conceived. Like sex.

He had turned around by this time, finishing up the dishes, and the more Kinley sipped her wine and thought about conception, the greater his ass began to look. Well, it *had* been a long time since she'd last had sex and she was a normal, virile young woman just like any other. As the wine loosened her inhibitions, she was starting to think of ways she could get him into bed. *Oh, my... my shirt fell off.* No, too obvious. How about, *I'm not wearing any underwear beneath my pants?* Still too obvious. She wondered how he would react if she just walked up to him and laid a big kiss right on him. They'd kissed before and the sparks had flown hard and fast.

That wasn't the only thing she wanted hard and fast from him.

But she kept her mouth shut, watching his butt as he finished with the dishes. She was content just doing that as he rattled on about the house back in the days of the Indian Wars. Something about arrowheads still embedded in the exterior walls, but Kinley wasn't really listening as she mentally undressed him. When he put the last one into the dishwasher, he pulled a paper towel off of the roll and turned to look at her.

"How about that tour now?" he said.

Kinley was all for the tour. And possibly all for watching his great ass as it walked in front of her, pointing out the home features. Pouring herself a third glass of wine, she followed him through the house as he explained that the living room had once been the entire downstairs living space. It had a massive stone fireplace, made from river rock, and wide pine floors.

There had been a loft upstairs that had eventually been turned into two bedrooms and a bathroom. Then there was the dining room that used to be part of the porch and the master bedroom which had been added on some-time during the mid-part of the last century. All in all, it was a great house with some great features and Kinley liked it a great deal. She was also coming to like Reed a great deal. All of her reservations about the man seemed to be vanishing, dashed away by his persistence and kindness. She'd never known anyone like him. He was incredibly hot and a good cook to boot. The wine was pumping through her veins at this point and her self-control was gone. She wanted Reed in the worst possible way. As he paused to point up at the beams in the exposed dining room ceiling,

Kinley put her hands on his face and attached herself to his lips.

It was a swift and bold move from the woman who had never, since Reed had known her, taken an aggressive or proactive stance when it came to him. He'd been the one to do all of the chasing. When she slanted her wine-tasting lips over his, he didn't even hesitate to respond. Maybe in hindsight, given her fragile mental state, he should have. But his lust had the best of him and he wrapped his big arms around her, matching her kiss for kiss, taste for taste, as they explored each other as they'd never done before. Reed was caught up in the tornado of passion just like Kinley was and when she went for his belt buckle, it never occurred to stop her. He didn't want to stop her. She unfastened his belt as he loosened her top.

Things began to fall to the floor. His belt, her top, then his shirt left a trail from the dining room, through the kitchen, and into the master bedroom. By the time he lifted her up and put her on the bed, her bra was coming off and he tossed it aside, latching on to her hard nipples and listening to her gasp. The pants were next and he slipped them off of her as his came next.

She was warm and soft and sweet, everything he knew she would be. He couldn't remember the last time he'd had sex but even if he could, it didn't compare to what was happening at this moment. It was as if everything he'd ever hoped for and dreamed about was here, right in his hands, and he took it happily. He'd wanted this woman since nearly the moment he first met her and the rewards of those wishes were greater than he had imagined.

On the bed, on the messy sheets, he lay down on top of her, wedging himself between her legs, which spread eagerly for him. With his mouth fused to hers, his hands began to move, touching her everywhere, feeling the texture of her skin before he would smell it and then taste it. Her nipples drew his gaze and he suckled her gently, listening to her pants of pleasure.

Reed took his time with her, at least he tried to, but his lust had the better of him. In little time, he thrust into Kinley as she groaned with pleasure, lifting her legs to welcome him deep as their bodies fused in the primal mating ritual. He thrust into her tight body repeatedly, feeling more pleasure than he ever imagined possible as she responded to him intuitively. As if she knew what he liked and how he liked it. Reed took her once on her back, stretched up over her, and then turned her over and took her a second time as she lay on her belly.

It was magic.

Reed was able to withdraw in time for his first climax but not for his second. He wasn't thinking about pulling out, only of the extreme pleasure he was experiencing. When he realized he'd come inside of her, he didn't miss a stroke because there was no use in pulling out at that point. Kinley didn't say a word about it. No scolding, no freaking out. In fact, when he came inside of her, she had two very powerful orgasms, one after the other, the cries of which were drowned out in the pillow.

Emotionally and physically exhausted, Reed moved his weight off of her body, pulling Kinley against him as he held her tightly. Eventually, he heard her doze off again, softly snoring, while he remained staring off into the darkness of the room and never feeling as close to anyone as he did to her at this moment. Oddly enough, his conversation with Beau came back to him.

If it's meant to be... she'll come to you.

She had.

As the night around them deepened, he finally slept.

EIGHT

OH, *God... what have I done?*

Kinley was staring up at the ceiling of Reed's master bedroom, listening to him snore deeply and evenly. He was in a dead sleep, his arm around her torso possessively, a hand still on her breast. Every so often he would squeeze it, gently. It was those squeezes that had invited non-stop sex for the past several hours. He loved her breasts and it was obvious. Being that the wine had made her extremely horny, Kinley had given in to every touch, every kiss, and Reed wasn't shy about sharing his. He was a generous lover and Kinley was fairly certain she'd had more orgasms in one sex session than she'd ever had in her life at one time. It hadn't been hard with him.

It had been some of the best sex of her life.

But now, she was lying awake as he slept, absolutely terrified of the man because she was quite sure she'd fallen in love with him. What wasn't to love? He was handsome, sweet, kind, and had the patience of Job. He'd done all he could to be compassionate and understanding with her as she worked through her many fears and phobias. He could have walked away at any time – in fact, he *should* have walked away at any time. No man in his right mind would have kept pursuing her after the crazy things she had done.

But Reed had.

Which made things worse. He was a sweet, normal guy without any hang-ups and she was a basket case. Well, at least she had been, but the past couple of days had seen vast improvements in that area thanks to Reed. He'd helped her grieve in a way she hadn't wanted to, openly and painfully, but he'd been there to hold together the pieces when she was in danger of falling apart. What kind of guy did that? A very special one. A very special guy who didn't need a woman with the kind of baggage she had.

But she loved him and that thought was terrifying enough. The last people she'd loved had been killed, ripping her guts out and leaving a great big hole in her. She was terrified to love, terrified to feel, but Reed had made her feel something she thought she'd lost. Turning her head slightly, she could see him as he lay on his belly, his face half-buried in the pillow. He looked so peaceful. Very carefully, she disengaged his arm from her torso and climbed out of bed.

Her clothes were all over the house, it seemed. She found her bra and pants in the bedroom but her shoes and shirt outside in the hall. The big dogs were sleeping in the hallway outside, lifting their heads to look at her as she tiptoed by. Her clothing was back on, she found her purse in the kitchen, and the house phone, and quietly called information for a taxi service. There was no local taxi service but there was a ride-share service, so she called that number. A driver was promised within a half hour, so gathering her things, she crept out of the house, into the dead of night, to wait by the main gate for the driver.

As she waited in the cold and darkness, she tried not to feel guilty for leaving Reed without telling him why. *I'm in love with the guy*, she thought. *I can't love him and burden him with all of this baggage I have. It isn't fair.* She'd been avoiding him and sneaking out on him since they'd first met, so this wasn't any different. Maybe this time he'd finally get the hint and leave her alone for good. It was better for him that way. But something told her to expect a visit from him in the morning.

She was right.

After an hour of sleep, maybe, Kinley was at The Coffee Cakery before dawn, opening it up for her employees. The sous chef and the line cook and a couple of the kitchen workers went inside, into the kitchen, to begin preparing for the day, as Kinley went back to her office.

She was settling down to do some paperwork when she heard some voices in the front of the house. It didn't concern her in the least because she knew the cooks were up there and people would soon be arriving for work, but suddenly, the cooks were all in her office and there were two men with shotguns following close behind. Her heart sank at the sight.

It was a robbery.

It was pretty early in the morning for this kind of thing which told Kinley that the robbers must have been staking the place out. This time, however, she didn't have a rifle underneath her desk that she could use to defend everyone with. She had a handgun in the bottom drawer but couldn't get to it without them seeing her move. But there was a gun in the safe. If she could only get them to have her open the safe, she might have a chance. The man who seemed to be doing all of the shoving and talking had on a baseball cap, a bandana over his nose and mouth, and a sawed-off shotgun.

"Stand up, lady," he told her, pointing the gun in her direction. "I hate to ruin your morning, but we need something from you."

Kinley put her hands up slowly as she rose from her chair. "Okay," she said steadily. "But don't hurt anyone. There's nothing here worth anyone dying for."

The other guy with a shotgun, wearing a military-looking knit hat pulled down over his ears, reached out to grab her by the arm.

"That depends on how you look at it," he said. "Where's the safe?"

Kinley didn't like being yanked around. "It's here in my office," she said. "In the closet over there. But if the manager followed protocol, he took yesterday's receipts to the bank last night. There will only be a couple of hundred dollars in it."

The guy let go of her hand and jabbed the shotgun at her. "Open it."

Kinley sighed faintly and opened the closet, leaning over to get a better look at the combination lock on the safe. She tried to position her body so that the robber with the shotgun pointed at her back couldn't get a look at what was inside the safe because once she got the gun in her hand, he was the first one she was going to take out. The robber, however, had other ideas; he was rather turned on by the woman's ass in his face and he reached out to put a hand on it.

"Nice," he commented, snorting lewdly.

Kinley kicked back at him, right in the knee, and the guy grunted in pain as he nearly dropped the shotgun. Kinley spun around with the intention of grabbing it but the robber was a hair faster than she was. He held the end up into her face and Kinley literally found herself looking down the barrel.

"Don't do that again!" the guy yelled. "I swear to God I'll kill you next time."

Kinley didn't back down, angry and frightened now. "Then don't *you* touch me again, or the next time I kick, it'll be aimed at your balls," she snarled. "Get it?"

The guy shoved the barrel closer to her face. "Open the fucking safe!"

Furious, Kinley turned back to the safe, knowing she had to get her hands on that gun right off the bat. If she didn't, she suspected things might go very badly for them all. But she remained cool, her hand steady, as she began to work the combination of the safe. The guy behind her with the shotgun aimed at her head spoke quietly.

"You and I are going to spend some time in this office when this is over," he said suggestively. "Hurry up with that safe."

Kinley knew exactly what he meant. Heart pounding against her ribs, she dialed the last number on the safe and it popped open. As she pulled the door open, she could see the handle of the gun tucked against the side of the safe and she immediately grabbed for it, throwing herself to the floor of the closet as she spun around, hoping to avoid most of the shotgun spray. She knew at this range, however, she was bound to catch some of it so she simply tried to keep her head down.

Lifting the gun, she fired off one round when the entire world exploded.

———

She'd left him. Again.

After what was inarguably the best sex of his life, Reed awoke to an empty bed unless he wanted to count the dogs that had crept in to sleep with him when Kinley opened the door. His German Shepherd was snoring very happily next to his head, but no Kinley.

Goddammit!

Now he was just plain angry. Angry because he knew they had something wonderful going last night, one of the best nights of his life, and he knew she felt it, too. They'd had such a great time sharing dinner and conversation, and then the sex… she had instigated it and as he got up out of bed, he suspected she left because she was ashamed and frightened at having been so wild. Maybe she had awoken to a bad case of regrets. In any case, he wasn't going to let her get away with it.

He wasn't going to let *her* get away.

So he took a quick shower and shaved, and pulled on his uniform that was still hanging in the dry cleaners bags in the closet. All the while, he was thinking about what he was going to say to Kinley when he showed up at The Coffee Cakery. *Hi, honey… I love you?* Well, it was to the point because he did. He had been in love with the woman since nearly the day he'd met her even though she had been a basket case and continued to be.

So what made him love her? He wasn't exactly sure, but it had something to do with the look in her eyes on that day at the Hi-Way Café that seemed so long ago. She had been cool, steady, calm, and brave. So maybe it was the bravery that he loved. Or maybe it was the silly giggle she had, or the moments of brilliance he saw when she came out of her shell. Or maybe it was just the feeling of her in his hands last night when they had made love. It still made him hot to think about it and, like it or not, they were going to explore it together. Frightened or ashamed, he didn't care what she felt. He was going to soothe it, smooth it over, or whatever he had to do in order to work her through this.

He wasn't about to let her go.

So he put on his Sam Browne and pulled on his duty jacket, set the alarm, and left the house to the patrol car that was still parked outside. He couldn't imagine how she got a ride back to Riverton but she somehow must have because there were tire tracks in the dirt outside of his security gate that he didn't recognize. Throwing the car into drive, he took off to Riverton.

The sun was just starting to come up as he entered the town. He thought about stopping to get coffee at his favorite coffee house but decided against it. He was going to have coffee at The Coffee Cakery and make Kinley pay for it in punishment for running out on him. For running out on *them*. He just wasn't going to let her run any longer.

Therefore, he pulled up to The Coffee Cakery in stealth, like he usually did, because the sight of his unit might send her into hiding. He pulled up across the street where he normally sat, beneath the trees that camouflaged his vehicle, so he could see most of the parking lot towards the rear and the front door at the same time. When he first arrived, there was no one there, but soon Kinley's non-descript Toyota pulled up, followed quickly by two more cars that parked near her.

Kinley got out of the car and his heart leapt at the sight of her. Only an idiot in love would feel like that over a woman who had been running from him since the moment he met her. He grinned to himself as he watched her cross the parking lot with a few employees, disappearing from his view when she went to the back door to open the place up.

Another employee arrived and he saw Kinley as she unlocked the front door of the restaurant. He figured now would be a good time to go in and hash it out with her, before her day officially began and before more employees arrived, but just as he began to pull his car out of his hiding spot, another car pulled into the parking lot and he saw two young men get out. He thought they were more employees until one young man pulled a shotgun out from beneath his coat. Both young men were heavily dressed as they headed for the back door and disappeared from sight.

Startled by what he had just seen, Reed had a split second of disbelief before his training kicked in. He immediately called for backup but he knew he couldn't wait for them. Whatever was going down, Kinley was inside and he couldn't sit by while she faced an imminent threat. He had to get in there to help her.

Just like she had once saved him, now, he had to save her.

Bailing from the car, he ran across the street.

Reed ended up in the shadows of the building, peering around the front to see if he could see any movement. He caught the tail-end of the robbers moving the people in the front of the restaurant toward the back, now both of the robbers with shotguns. They were moving toward the back door where Kinley's office was. He then moved swiftly down the side of the building, waving off a few more employees who just arrived, signaling for them to get back into their cars and leave, which they hurriedly did. Whenever a deputy with his service weapon out gives an order, the command is not meant to be disobeyed.

The employees scattered.

With the employees gone, Reed peeked around the side of the building and could see the back door, but there was no movement. The door remained shut. He paused a split second longer to see if the door moved at all, but it didn't, so he raced to the back door, keeping his back pressed up against the side of the building. There was a glass panel in the door, protected by safety bars, and he rolled slightly in the direction of the door so he could catch a glimpse inside. Kinley's office was right by the back door and he could see that her door was partially open. He had two of her cooks in his line of sight and they had their hands up.

So it goes down in her office, he thought grimly. He could hear some yelling at that point; someone was unhappy. Unhappiness during a robbery was never a good thing. He could hear sirens coming in the distance and it infuriated him. He specifically told dispatch to roll officers Code Two. If the robbers heard the sirens, it would spook them and he feared what would happen. At that point, he had no choice. He had to move.

Carefully, he opened the back door and one of the cooks caught the movement and turned to look at him. Reed quickly held a finger up to his lips, a gesture of silence, and the cook fearfully turned around to pretend he hadn't seen him. The air was full of anxiety as Reed entered the back hall, pressing himself against the wall and staying clear of the door. He was about to move when he heard a round being fired inside the room. With no more time to waste, he kicked the door open wide about the time a shotgun blast took out several ceiling tiles.

The blast had come from a man falling backwards, a man with a shotgun in his hand. As the man fell on to his back, Reed caught sight of another man with a shotgun aimed right at him. Reed threw himself out of the doorway, back into the hall, as a shotgun blast ripped out part of the door jamb. But then he was back in the doorway, as quick as a flash, his service revolver firing and taking out the man who had just fired at him. As that man went down, the man on the floor rolled to his knees but he wasn't able to bring his gun up before someone from the closet put a bullet in his brain. He fell to the floor like a stone, bleeding out on the carpet.

Reed still had his gun out, leveled at the cooks now. "Is that all there is?" he demanded. "Are there any more of them?"

The cooks shook their heads, all in a panic. "No!" one guy yelled, "Just two that we saw."

Reed kept his gun leveled for a moment longer before lowering it, taking a moment to survey the carnage of the room. Outside the back door, he could hear police sirens blaring as deputies began to run in through the door, weapons brandished.

Reed called them off.

"All clear," he said, turning to see two wide-eyed deputies in the doorway. "Get these guys out of here. Make sure they're okay and then we need statements. And someone get on the radio and get my dad down here. We're going to need him."

The deputies began moving, pulling the cooks out of the office as Reed went to the closet where Kinley was just sitting up. Their eyes met and a thousand emotions filled the air between them. It was a cavalcade of angst and relief and joy.

Reed was the first one to speak.

"Are you okay?" he asked calmly. "Did they hurt you?"

Kinley had never been so glad to see anyone in her entire life. "No," she said. "Thank God you came when you did."

Reed simply nodded, his jaw ticking as he holstered his weapon. He was trying very hard to remain calm, to think deliberately and to speak deliberately. But it was hard to keep the emotion out of the equation so he simply gave up.

"I was only here because you left without a word," he said, looking at her and trying not to feel hurt. "I came to see you like I always do when you run out on me, Kinley. You've been running out on me since the day we met and I came to tell you that I'm not chasing you anymore. You've made it clear that you don't want anything to do with me, so I'm going to respect your wishes this time."

Kinley didn't say anything at first. It was a gut punch, but one she deserved. She knew that. Slowly, she stood up, brushing off her black pants.

"I don't think this is the time to discuss this, Reed," she

finally said. "Let me get through interrogation for this and then we can discuss it if you want to."

He shook his head, pulling out his pad of paper and pen. "No need," he said. "I've said all I needed to say."

He had his head down as he began to write. The conversation was decisively over. Verging on tears, Kinley walked past him, into the corridor outside her office, and straight into the bathroom. Shutting the door, she bolted it and promptly vomited. Everything in her stomach and probably everything she'd eaten over the past week came out and then some. And when she was finished vomiting, she sat back against the wall and burst into tears.

Painful tears.

It wasn't because of the attempted robbery. She'd long grown tough to something like that. Sure, it had scared her, but she came out all right and so had her employees. That's all that mattered in the end. The pain was because of the agony in Reed's face when he told her he wasn't going to chase her anymore. She wasn't sure what she expected when she ran away from him yet again, but he'd finally taken a stand. She was proud of him.

But she was not proud of what she'd done.

She couldn't stay here anymore.

It was time to move on.

NINE

NO ONE HAD SEEN Kinley leave the scene of the crime.

She didn't know where Reed was, but she assumed he was somewhere in the restaurant. Quietly, and quickly, she made her way out to her car and sped off toward the house her brother had purchased for her. The closer she drew to the small, two-bedroom home that had been built in the early part of the last century, the more she started to realize this wasn't a situation she could run away from again. Her instinct, the flight or fight, was telling her to stay and fight. Too often she'd given in to the flight part. But this time, it was different.

This time, something was telling her to fight.

Fight for Reed.

By the time she got home, she was mentally and physically exhausted. She knew that the cops were going to want to interview her, but that didn't stop her from stripping down and getting into the bathtub. Swamped by the hot water, she lay there and stared at the wall.

She had some decisions to make.

Clearly, she couldn't keep running. She'd built up a life here and a successful business and she didn't want to walk away from it. Her instinct of self-preservation was screaming at her to keep running, but no matter where she would run, her past would catch up to her. Everything would catch up to her.

She couldn't spend her life like that.

As she lay there, thoughts of her children came flooding back. Yesterday, with Reed, was the first time she'd spoken of them since it happened. Years of keeping her children buried, tucked deep inside and forgotten. Secrets she'd never meant to reveal. Was that fair to them? Fair that their own mother had tried to forget them? Tears began to run down her face as she thought of Vi and Liam. She could still hear Vi's laughter and see the impish look in Liam's eyes when he was doing something he knew he shouldn't be doing.

Was it fair to bury them forever and forget them?

No, it really wasn't.

And what about her husband?

Tom had been a good guy. A cop, just like her. They'd laughed together a lot. She missed his crazy sense of humor, but there were things in Reed that reminded her of Tom. The dedication to duty, the way he spoke to her. Calmly, sometimes sweetly, but always honestly. Tom did that, too. Maybe that's why she'd been attracted to Reed in the first place and maybe why he freaked her out from time to time. She felt such comfort with him, such peace, but then her subconscious would remember having that comfort and peace ripped away, so she'd bolt. Self-protection was in overdrive.

But she couldn't do it anymore.

She had to acknowledge the past.

Climbing out of the tub, she dried off and got dressed. She brushed her hair back into a loose ponytail and put on some makeup. For a moment, she gazed at herself in the mirror, mentally preparing for what she needed to do.

Kinley Connors-Berrington needed to grow up.

It was time.

She picked up her cell phone, found a number in her contacts, and dialed.

The callee picked up on the second ring.

"Kin?"

Kinley heard the voice, fighting the urge to weep when she did. "Hey," she said. "Before you panic, everything is okay. In fact... I wanted to talk to you about something. Are you busy?"

"Never for you," the man said. "What's on your mind?"

"Well," Kinley started. "First off, I wanted to thank you for being the best brother ever. You've got above and beyond, Ethan. You've covered for me, kept my secrets... and I don't think I've ever thanked you."

On the other end of the line, Ethan Connors smiled. "You're welcome," he said. "But I have to say, you scared the shit out of me right now. You never call me unless something is going on."

"Something is going on," Kinley said. "I think... I think I'm ready to come back to the land of the living."

"You mean come home?"

"Maybe," she said. "Etie, I never asked you anything about Mom or Dad or the funeral or anything. You tried to tell me a few times, but I hung up on you. I'm sorry I did that. But I wasn't ready to face it yet."

Etie. The name she'd given him in childhood, the name for a brother who was eighteen months older than she was. He hadn't heard that name in years.

"I know," he said. "It took me a while to realize that. Hey, why the change in heart? What's going on?"

Kinley thought about how much to tell him but quickly decided she'd tell him everything. She'd held secrets far too long as it was.

"It's a bit of a story," she said. "Do you have a minute?"

"I just closed my office door. You've got me for as long as you need me."

Ethan was a lawyer in a high-powered Los Angeles law firm. He'd done well for himself. He settled back down in his chair just as his sister began to talk.

She went back to the beginning at the Hi-Way Café, where she'd lost the baby she'd been carrying and was trying to decide how to kill herself. She told him that she ended up working at that stale, dirty café and the day Reed McCoy came into her life. She told him about running to Riverton and trying to start a new life, and how Reed had found her there. She told him about the robbery attempt that morning and what Reed had said to her. What he'd meant to her before that. In an hour and a half-long conversation, Kinley told her brother everything.

It all came out.

She came clean.

When she was finished, Ethan seemed to be rather stunned. For a moment, he didn't say a word. Then, he finally sighed.

"Damn," he muttered. "I had no idea, Kin."

"I know."

"But Reed is right. You did treat him like shit."

Kinley was laying on her couch by this time, phone to her ear. "I did," she said. "But I told you why. He does not need to get mixed up with someone like me. I'm like a lightning rod for bad luck."

"Did you ever stop to think that he's exactly what you need?"

"But I'm not exactly what he needs."

"Kin, you're not thinking this through," he said. "You're throwing up roadblocks when there is someone who clearly wanted to be with you and help you grow in spite of knowing everything about you. He *knows* your past."

Kinley was starting to get teary-eyed. "Yes, he does," she said, sniffling. "But what I didn't tell you is that I do love him. I'm so afraid I'm going to hurt him if we're together."

"You've already hurt him and he keeps coming back,"

Ethan pointed out. "He seems something in you that you don't see in yourself."

"What's that?"

"That there *is* something redeemable about you. That you're worth saving."

Kinley hadn't thought of it that way. Tears streamed down her temples as she thought on her brother's words.

"The past few years have been hell," she whispered tightly. "I haven't let myself feel anything for fear of what would happen if I did. I'd remember the pain, the grief, the loss. I hate him for making me feel those things, but I love him for making me feel those things."

"Have you told him?"

"No."

"You should," Ethan said. "Don't let this relationship end without telling him what he's meant to you. That's not fair to him."

She thought on that for a moment. "You're right," she said. "Etie?"

"What?"

"How are Mom and Dad?"

He sighed again, heavily this time. "Kin, I'll tell you what you want to know," he said. "But don't you dare call them to talk to them only to disappear again. They couldn't take it. Do you understand me?"

"Of course I do," she said. "Why? What's wrong?"

"Mom's been having heart issues," he said. "They put a pacemaker in about six months ago."

Kinley sat up from the couch. "Oh, my God," she said, hand on her mouth. "Is she okay?"

Ethan grunted. "You know, I could get really pissed off about that question and ask you why do you even care," he said. "You left us, remember? That doesn't give you the right to care about the people you left behind. Not when you fucked us all over when we were dealing with the death of Vi and Liam and Tom."

Those were extremely harsh words and Kinley had to resist the urge to bite back at him, but she didn't. He was right. But his words still hurt, true though they might be.

"You're absolutely right," she said. "So I can do one of two things here. I can hang up this phone and never contact you again, or I can come home and apologize and try to reestablish relationships. I didn't leave because I wanted to, Ethan. I left because if I didn't, I was going to kill myself. I was going to blow my brains out and Mom and Dad would have had to deal with that. So I left. I ran from that person who wanted to put a gun to her head. I ran from them telling me that Violet tried to defend herself against the bullets that came flying at her. I ran from them telling me that Liam was drawing a picture when death came for him and they found it in his hand. A little, bloody picture in his little, bloody hand. Everyone grieves differently, Ethan, so don't you judge me. Don't you fucking judge me."

"I'm not, I'm not," Ethan said quickly, backing down. "If I was judging you, I wouldn't have kept your secret. But I have always hoped you would come around and make things right. You left us to grieve your entire family, alone. We didn't even have you with us. I guess... I guess I just get mad when I think about Mom and Dad visiting Vi and Liam's grave every Sunday and telling them how proud their mommy is of them. It should be *you* doing that, Kin. Not them."

Kinley burst into tears. "Oh, my God, you're right," she sobbed. "You're absolutely right. I need to come home to see my babies and apologize for what I did. But... but I just didn't know what else to do. I just didn't know."

"I'm sorry," Ethan said softly. "I didn't mean to make you cry. If you want to come home, tell me when and I'll pick you up at the airport. I'll do whatever you need me to do. But I have a confession to make."

"What?" she wept.

"Mom and Dad know about you," he said. "Mom saw our text string when she went to use my phone one time. So, she knew. She's always said you'd come back when you were ready."

Kinley wiped at her face, struggling with her composure. "I'm ready," she said. "I have a few things to take care of here, but I'm ready. I'll call you when I book my flight."

On the other end of the line, Ethan closed his eyes tightly, fighting off the relief and joy he was feeling. "Okay," he said. "I'm really glad to hear this. You have no idea."

"Actually, I think I kind of do."

"Can I tell Mom and Dad?"

"You'd better. I don't want to surprise them and give them both heart attacks when I walk through the door."

"Good call."

"I'll call you in the next day or two and let you know."

"Sounds good," Ethan said. "Love you, Kin."

"Love you, too. And thank you."

Ending the call, Kinley sat for a moment, thinking of the loose ends she needed to tie up before heading back to Los Angeles. She rather liked her life in Riverton, so she wasn't sure she was going to move back any time soon, but she had to go back. She had to acknowledge what had happened, she had to grieve it properly, and she had to see her children.

No more running.

Kinley was going home.

TEN

FOUR DAYS since the attempted robbery, The Coffee Cakery was back to business as usual. It was standing room only and a line out the door, and on this bright morning, the smell of coffee and cinnamon was heavy in the air.

The place was hopping.

Kinley was back in her usual spot, at the counter making sure the orders were taken out in a timely manner as she chattered with the counter customers. News of the attempted robbery has spread all over town so that was all anyone wanted to talk about. Mostly, they just wanted to make sure Kinley and her staff hadn't been injured, so she'd spent all morning reassuring people that she was just fine, the cooks were just fine, and everything was just fine in general.

But in the back parking lot, trouble was brewing.

A new restaurant was going in down the street and the construction workers were not at all shy about parking in

Kinley's lot and blocking in her employees or taking their parking spaces. That had been going on for the past three days and, finally, Kinley had enough of it. Placing a call to the sheriff's department code enforcement, she went back to the counter and mentioned her call to the manager. The guy nodded in agreement, rolling his eyes, as another order came up and, with the waitress busy, Kinley picked up the French toast and egg white omelet.

It was for an outside table and she headed out into the sunshine, locating the table with two people and putting their food in front of them. She was heading back inside when she caught a glimpse of a sheriff's unit making the turn onto the street that paralleled the restaurant, so she headed to the rear of the establishment.

Her heart was in her throat. She was fairly certain it wouldn't be Reed. In fact, she was positive. She hadn't seen the man in four days, not since fleeing after the attempted robbery. She'd even gone to the sheriff's station to sit through questioning with the detectives, and Reed hadn't shown himself once. She knew why. Of course she knew why.

But it was still like a stab to the gut.

Kinley had decided, after the epiphany phone call with her brother, that she wasn't going to go crawling back to Reed. She'd already done that and it had ended badly – for him. She wasn't going to turn the guy into a human yo-yo more than she already had because it simply wasn't fair to him. She loved him enough not to do that to him.

But it didn't make it hurt any less.

Coming out of the back door of the restaurant, she saw the sheriff's unit pull in. She was halfway to it when a very big man she recognized climbed out and put on his regulation cowboy hat. Dumbfounded that Reed had come on the call, Kinley stood there, unsure what to say to the man. Her heart was beating a mile a minute. But she quickly decided to simply be all-business with him. There wasn't any reason not to be. Especially if they were going to live, and work, in the same area.

But all of that resolve nearly went out the window when he looked up and saw her. Kinley took a deep breath and forced a smile as he came around the front of the car in her direction.

"Hi," she said. "I'm so sorry to be a bother, but we've got more parking issues and I didn't want it turn into a big battle, so I thought I'd better take care of it now."

He was looking at his pad, writing something. "What's the problem?"

Kinley began to point to the various cars. "Those aren't my employees," she said. "They're construction workers from down the street. You know that restaurant they're remodeling?"

"A few doors down?"

"That one," she said. "They started parking here a couple of days ago, taking our spots and then blocking my employees in when they couldn't find a place."

He began to look around. In fact, other than getting out of his car, he couldn't seem to look at her at all.

"Do you want to flag them for me so I know?" he said.

Kinley nodded, rushing back into the restaurant and emerging shortly with a Post-It pad. She waded out into the cars and began sticking a bright yellow piece of paper on the cars that didn't belong to the restaurant. All the while, Reed kept writing. Then, he put the notepad away and pulled out his ticket book.

Silently, he went to ticket.

The silence between them was painful. Kinley wasn't sure what to say to him and it was clear that he didn't want to talk to her. Not that she blamed him. But she also didn't want him to go the rest of his life thinking that she was a horrible person who didn't care who she hurt. Still, she couldn't fault him for just doing his job and nothing more. No conversation, no hint that the two of them had ever spoken of love.

Without another word, she retreated back into the restaurant.

———

The call was his.

He was covering Steve Turner's patrol area on that morning, which included the main drag and The Coffee Cakery. Chances were that he wasn't going to get a call there, or be forced to see Kinley, until that call came through and his stomach dropped. He probably could have gotten someone else to take it, but he didn't. He should have, but he didn't.

He'd just spent four days in hell.

Hell that was only going to get worse if he didn't cut himself loose from Kinley. At least cut himself loose from the memories of her, the feel of her, the taste of her. The night of the attempted robbery at the restaurant, he'd sat in the breakroom for five hours with Turner, giving him a rundown of his entire relationship with Kinley from the moment he met her until the moment he walked away from her after saving her ass at the restaurant. Steve was sympathetic, but he kept saying the same thing over and over.

You dodged a bullet with her, dude.

While that was potentially true, Reed still didn't think so. According to everything he'd read about Kinley, and everything she told him, she wasn't a flake by nature. She'd led a perfectly normal, ordinary life until the gang bangers took out her family. After that, her history was sketchy – a woman struggling to deal with grief, unable to cope, and unsure how to get her life back. That was really all he saw. He wanted to help her, and he had tried, but the truth was the couldn't fix someone who wasn't ready to be fixed. Kinley was still grieving and there was nothing he could do to change that, though he'd tried. He'd tried harder than he ever had, with anyone.

And he'd failed.

He was a man who didn't often fail.

She was grieving, now he was hurting, but it was his own damn fault. Even he knew that. She'd been clear with him from the very start and he'd ignored her and just charged full steam ahead, like he could force her to his will.

Like he could force her to become what he wanted her to become – a woman who had dealt with her grief and was ready to move on with her life. He didn't blame her. In fact, he had never blamed her.

This was on him.

His stomach was in knots as he pulled up on the restaurant and even more in knots when he saw her standing just outside the back door. She'd smiled at him, timidly, and he hadn't even responded. He couldn't. He was afraid that if he smiled, he'd be begging for her forgiveness for what he said to her and that would ruin everything. He wasn't sorry for what he'd said, only that he'd had to say it.

Once she told him what the trouble was, he went about his business without another word. He was acutely aware when she went back inside the restaurant. He felt as if he could breathe a little now that she wasn't nearby, but he also felt sad that she had gone away. He took his time finishing up what he was doing because he needed to go inside to give her some information about it, something he was dreading to do. He couldn't even look at the woman, so he wasn't sure how he was going to hold a conversation with her.

Maybe he should have had someone take this call, after all.

Tickets finished, he headed inside and found her in her office, which had been cleaned up since the incident four days ago. The blood stains on the wall were gone and it smelled like bleach. When Kinley saw him, she stood up from behind her desk as he came into the office.

"I ticketed the cars because they're on private property, and you have it properly posted, but you really need to get your employees parking permits," he said. "I noticed some of them don't have any and the next time, it may not be me who comes. Everybody is going to get a ticket."

He was looking at her as he spoke, not even making the connection that she was going over to the office door and shutting it. When he realized that, he let out a grunt and averted his gaze.

"I need to go, Kinley," he said quietly. "I'm covering two patrol districts today, so I can't stay."

She didn't move away from the door. "You can stay long enough for me to thank you," she murmured. "Reed, you were right about everything. I've had a long talk with my brother and tomorrow, I'm flying back to Los Angeles to face the things I couldn't face before. You gave me that strength and I wanted to say thank you in case... well, in case I don't ever see you again. You tolerated a woman who treated you like shit and you did it with grace and understanding. I can never repay you for that kindness, so I wanted you to know that I'm grateful."

By this time, he was looking at her seriously. "You're moving back to L.A.?"

She shook her head. "Probably not," she said. "But I don't know how long I'll be gone. I need to see my mom and dad. I need to see my brother, my friends. But most of all, I need to see my kids and tell them... tell them how much I loved them and how proud I was of them. How sorry I am that I wasn't there when they were put in the ground. There's just a lot I need to say to them."

She was starting to tear up, fighting against that gut-tearing grief, but she was holding her own. She was trying very hard. He knew how difficult it was for her. Quite frankly, her decision surprised him but he wondered how much she meant it. She'd been known to run, or chicken out, even after she said she had made a decision because he'd been on the receiving end of that behavior.

He supposed that he would believe her if she really got on that plane.

"Good," he said after a moment. "I'm glad you're going to face it, I really am."

She shrugged. "I don't think I could have put the pieces of the puzzle together had you not helped me do that," she said. "I told my brother about you. He thinks you're one hell of a guy."

Reed averted his gaze again, uncomfortable and uncertain. "I'd do it all again for the woman who saved my life," he said. Then, he sighed slowly. "Knowing how this was going to end, I still wouldn't have changed a thing. How does that song go? I could have missed the pain but I would have had to miss the dance."

Kinley's tears were coming on strong. "Reed, I know I'm a giant, human red-flag," she said. "I know what I've done to you and to tell you I'm sorry just isn't enough. But know that I really am – I am sorry for running off, for eating your food, for sleeping with you and then running off again. I'm sorry for every hope I've given you that I turned around and shit on. But I think it took a lot of bumps and failures to come to the conclusion that I've come to. And the conclusion is that I don't want to be the person I've shown you. That's why I'm going back to L.A. I need to find the Kinley I left behind when I ran."

He was looking at her once again, his hazel eyes glimmering. "I think she's one hell of a woman."

"How would you know?"

"I've read the articles about you," he said. "I know all about your service record from those. And I've seen glimpses of that woman from time to time. It would be nice to meet that person one day, for good."

Kinley nodded, looking at her feet, before she stood aside and opened the door for him. When he looked at her with an expression that suggested he knew she was trying to kick him out and their conversation had come to an end, she spoke very softly.

"One more thing," she said, unable to look at him. "Reed, I love you. In spite of everything, I have fallen in love with you. After everything that's happened, I don't expect you to return that sentiment or even believe me. I'm not sure even *I* would believe me. But I'm flying out of Casper in two days on a United flight and if you want to come along... it seems to me that I can face this without you. It's not that I need you there, because I don't. But I believe you are responsible for getting me this far and it would seem a shame for you to not see it through. It would mean everything to me if you came, but I completely understand if you don't. And that's all I'm going to say about it."

With that, she put her hand on his arm, gave it a squeeze, and slipped past him. She headed towards the front of the restaurant as he stood there where she left him. With something of a stunned expression on his face, Reed forced himself to head out to his car.

The day, for him, had taken quite a turn.

Heading back to the station, he made a plan, too.

He had some phone calls to make.

<h1 style="text-align:center">ELEVEN</h1>

KINLEY MADE the flight to Los Angeles alone.

She had been hopeful he was going to board the plane up until they closed the door and secured it. After that, a massive sense of disappointment set in. He wasn't coming.

She really wasn't surprised.

She'd done a lot of thinking on that flight from Casper to Los Angeles, with a stop in Salt Lake City. The weather was good and she sat by the window, watching the clouds, watching the land below. So many people going about their lives, people who hadn't made a horrible incident worse like she had. More and more, she was coming to realize that she shouldn't have run, but grief was a funny thing. It caused people to behave in ways they wouldn't normally behave. Temporary insanity was more like it.

She had a lot of people to apologize to.

Her thoughts drifted back to her family and the house they'd lived in. California law declared a person legally dead if they were missing for five years, so she hadn't been declared legally dead yet. The house that she and Tom had owned had been in a trust, with her brother as executor, and he'd sold the house with her permission about two years ago. That's how she had the money to buy the home in Riverton and open up the restaurant in spite of what she'd told Reed. More secrets she kept from him, but it couldn't be helped.

A lot of things couldn't be helped.

But she was going to try.

Her parents lived in Pasadena, California and that was where she'd been raised. She knew they were still living in the house she grew up in because Ethan would have told her otherwise. Thinking about her childhood home brought tears to her eyes because it had been a place where she'd experienced so much with Tom and the kids. Christmases, birthdays... lots of memories there. But she was going to have to accept those memories and make peace with them. She didn't want to cry every time she went into her parents' house. The very people she had run from were going to have to help her with that. Her dad had always been the pragmatic sort. Reed may have gotten the ball rolling, but she was confident that her dad would help finish it.

Or, so she hoped.

However, as soon as the plane passed over the state line into California, she began to feel the pangs of anxiety. The last time Kinley saw California, it had been in her rear-view mirror as she spend away on the 15 freeway north. Looking down at the landscape, she recognized the Mojave desert, the parched hills and dales, and the Colorado River as it wound its way south. Sitting back in her seat, she couldn't watch anymore. She was drawing closer and closer to the scene of the most horrific moment in her life and she simply couldn't watch, but once the plane descended, she managed to peek out of the window to the familiar sights below.

The plane was near the San Gabriel mountains before making its turn to get into the landing pattern. She watched the 710 freeway pass below, the 110, and finally the 405. By that time, the plane was almost down and she closed her eyes as the tires hit the runway and the brakes were deployed.

She was really home.

Once the plane made it to the gate, Kinley sat there the longest time as the passengers disembarked, trying to summon the courage to get off with them. Doubts were clutching at her and she had to shrug them off and force herself to stand up when the last passengers filtered past her. One by one, the last of them got off until it was only the flight attendants.

The time had come.

Kinley had checked one bag and brought one carry on with her, so she slung her backpack purse on and pulled her small case out of the overhead bin. She was up near the front of the plane and was literally the last passenger off as the flight attendants bid her farewell. The smell of Los Angeles hit her in the nostrils full-force, the scent of jet fuel and beaches and smog. She found it incredibly comforting but also incredibly intimidating. It was a threat to her sanity.

To her everything.

But she sucked it up.

She was going to do this.

Kinley had told Ethan she'd meet him in baggage claim, so she made her way down to the familiar carousels. How many times had she been in this airport? Too many times to count. She knew it, and it knew her, silently welcoming her back to the land of her birth. Looking up at the displays, she discovered which carousel her luggage would be on and she made her way over to it. It wasn't ready yet and people were gathering, and as she texted her brother to tell him that she'd arrived, people began to stand around her, waiting for their luggage. She'd just put her phone away, feeling some impatience at the delayed luggage, when she heard a voice behind her.

"It's been a long time since I've been to L.A.."

It took Kinley a moment to recognize the voice and when she did, she spun around only to see Reed standing behind her. As her jaw dropped in astonishment, he grinned.

"Well?" he said. "You *did* invite me."

Kinley couldn't even speak. Suddenly, she was throwing herself at Reed, leaping up on the man and wrapping her arms round his neck as her mouth fused with his. Reed laughed low in his throat, his big arms going around her as she very nearly knocked him off balance. He ended up bumping into an older couple who laughed as both Reed and Kinley apologized. Reed ended up carrying her away from the carousel and to a corner that didn't have dozens people standing around.

He put her on her feet.

"You came," Kinley said, her eyes lit up with the joy she was feeling. "Oh, my God, I can't believe you came. I thought..."

"What did you think?"

"That you weren't coming."

He cocked an eyebrow. "Seriously?" he said. "The man who can't leave you alone no matter what he says wasn't going to come to California with you to face what you need to face? You *really* don't know me very well, Kinley."

She giggled weakly. "Now that you say it that way, it does sound ridiculous," she said. But she quickly sobered. "But after what you said to me... I thought you were through with me."

"Like I said, you don't know me very well."

Her gaze drifted over his face, studying his handsome features. "Maybe not, but I'm still glad to see you," she finally said. "Were you on the same flight with me?"

Reed shook his head. "You didn't tell me what flight you were on," he said. "I purchased a ticket for the first flight out this morning, but you weren't on it. So, I got here and just waited for you. I knew you'd come along eventually. At least, I hoped so. I wasn't entirely sure you wouldn't back out, in which case I'd be looking for a flight home tomorrow. But... you're here. Congratulations on making it this far."

She smiled weakly, looking around the terminal before she spoke. "It was hard to get off the plane," she admitted. "The memories... I was wondering all the way out here if I've made the right decision to come. But you... are *you* sure about this? I don't want you to wake up tomorrow and regret following me out here."

He lifted her hands to his lips and kissed them. "Look," he said with a sigh. "I've been wrestling with this ever since the attempted robbery. I joke about being the man who can't leave you alone, but it's true. Every instinct I have is telling me to walk away, but I just can't. I can't walk away from the woman who not only saved my life, but has become a big part of it. Tell me that I haven't made a mistake coming here, Kinley. That we're finally coming out of the woods on this. We've had a false start before. I can't do it again."

Kinley nodded quickly. "I can't, either," she said. "All I know is that *you* did this, Reed. You gave me the courage to get on a plane and come back to face my fears. You saw something in me that I don't, courage that I just don't think I have, but your faith in me has brought me here. Your faith gave me the courage."

He smiled faintly. "It was always there," he said. "You just had to remember it. I'm really proud of you for that. I know this isn't easy."

Kinley closed her eyes for a brief moment. "I can do this," she said. "Now that you're here, I can do anything."

"Whatever you need, I'm here for you," he said. Then, he paused. "But tell me again."

"Tell you what?"

"What you told me at the restaurant the last time I saw you."

She looked at him, puzzled. "What did I tell you?"

"That you love me."

Her smile grew and she leaned into him, wrapping her arms around him. "I do," she murmured. "Very much."

He swooped down for a big, juicy kiss. "I've been waiting my whole life to hear that."

"I think I've been waiting my whole life to say it."

He chuckled, kissing her one more time. "Say it as much as you want because I won't get sick of hearing it," he said. At that moment, the red rotating light lit up on the baggage carousel as the luggage began to come down the chute. He gestured at it. "Come on, let's get your stuff. What did you bring?"

"Just one piece," Kinley said, holding his hand as they walked over to the carousel. "It's pink leopard print."

"Of course it is."

She looked at him, laughing. "You didn't expect anything else, did you?"

"Nope."

He caught sight of the big, pink animal print suitcase as it came down the chute and he went over the edge of the carousel, heaving it up and taking it back over to where Kinley was standing. Now that she had all of her baggage, she began to look around for her brother.

"Ethan was supposed to meet me here," she said. "I don't know what kind of car he drives. I hope it's not a two-seater."

"Why?"

"Because unless you want me to sit on your lap, it won't fit all of us."

"Don't worry about it," Reed said. "I rented a car."

She looked at him, mildly surprised. "Why?" she asked. "You can come with us."

But he shook his head. "Honey, the focus needs to be on your family right now without me tagging along," he said. "You mentioned your folks live in Pasadena, so I've booked a room at the Langham there. This is a very important moment in your life, so focus on what you need to do with your parents and family. Mend the fences. I'll be here if you need me."

She was incredulous. "You flew out here just to be moral support?" she said. "Just hang around in case I need you?"

He shrugged. "You are going to need time alone with your family," he said. "When you feel – *if* you feel – like you want to introduce them to me, that's fine, but I wouldn't feel comfortable being part of the reunion. That's between you and your family."

She grew serious. "But you will come with me when I go to the cemetery, won't you?" she said. "I...I really want you to be there."

"If you want me to go, I will," he said.

She was still looking uncertain. "But what are you

going to do meanwhile?" she said. "Just hang around the hotel until I call you?"

He smiled. "I've got a good friend who lives in Pasadena," he said. "A guy I knew when I was with the CIA. We used to work together. I'm going to hang out with him. Trust me, I won't be bored."

"Will you at least miss me?"

He snorted. "With every breath I take," he said. Then, he glanced at his watch. "When did you say your brother was coming?"

She pulled out her phone and looked at it. "He's five minutes away."

"Okay," he said, leaning down to kiss her. "I'll go get the rental car and head to the hotel. I'll text you when I arrive."

"Can we have breakfast in the morning?"

"Anything you want. Just tell me where and I'll be there."

She nodded. "Okay," she said, then stood on her toes to kiss him one last time. "Reed... thank you again. I feel so much better with you here."

He winked at her. "Love you," he said. "I'll talk to you later."

Kinley watched him head out of baggage claim, toward curbside where the rental car buses were stopping every fifteen minutes or so. With a smile on her lips, Kinley collected her suitcase, her carry on, and her backpack purse and began to head out to the curb where her brother would be pulling up shortly. She was looking down the long curb, watching the blue rent-a-car bus pull away when a silver sports car pulled up in front of her.

Ethan Connors bailed out of his car as fast as his legs would carry him.

The tears of joy, for both Ethan and Kinley, were real and copious.

TWELVE

KINLEY'S first glimpse of the street she grew up on brought tears to her eyes. The jacaranda trees were in bloom this time of year and the entire street was lined with purple foliage. The house itself was mid-block, an English Tudor Revival built in 1933. As her brother drew closer, she could see two people standing on the lawn and she immediately recognized her parents. The tears started to flow and she was weeping by the time Ethan stopped the car. She didn't even have a chance to open her own door before her father was yanking it open and pulling her out of the passenger side.

Standing on the front lawn, in full view of the neighbors, Kinley and her parents were reunited.

There were tears and hugs, and more tears and more hugs. Ethan tried to herd them all into the house and they eventually made it inside, but it took a little doing. Kinley's father, a retired assistant sheriff for Los Angeles county, was probably the most emotional out of the four of them because in his long and storied career, he'd seen a lot of things. He knew what could happen to law enforcement officers, the threats they faced on a daily basis. The fact that it happened to his daughter was something he'd never gotten over.

There were a lot of things he hadn't gotten over.

It had been Bob Connors who had buried Violet and Liam Connors-Berrington. He was the one who had officially identified the children, and their father, at the crime scene. He was the one who had followed the coroner's van to the medical examiner's office, the one who had carried Liam out of the van and into the building because, by that time, he'd been informed that his daughter had driven off and no one could find her. He was terrified she'd gone to confront Mickey Mouse and his fellow gang members. He was furthermore terrified that she was going to be dead by the end of the day, so he stayed at the morgue, expecting his daughter to be brought in any moment.

But she never was.

By morning, no one could find her. Mickey Mouse and his colleagues had been arrested and booked, but there was no sign of Kinley. No one knew where she was. They tried tracing her credit card and there was a stop for gas outside of Las Vegas where she also drained as much money as she could out of her checking account, but after that, there was nothing. The going theory was that she'd been kidnapped by some of Mickey Mouse's friends and taken far, far away to be dumped.

Whatever the case, Kinley had vanished.

It was Bob who had stayed with his grandkids, as much as the medical examiner would let him, so they wouldn't be alone. Both kids were afraid of the dark and he tried to explain that to the coroner, who was genuinely sympathetic to the point of putting battery-operated stick-on lights in the drawers where the bodies were stored so there would be some light. Bob knew it was stupid, but he felt better about it, enough so that he went home after being awake for two straight days and slept for almost sixteen hours before returning to the medical examiner's office after the autopsies had been done. They hadn't let him in to witness the autopsies, though he had asked, but the medical examiner and his staff continued to make an exception when it came to Bob and his grandkids and let him see the reports as soon as they were done.

They'd given Bob nightmares for a solid year.

After that, it had been Bob and his wife, Linda, who had contacted the funeral homes and made the arrangements. Tom's parents wanted him buried with his grandparents at another cemetery and there was a bit of an argument about where the kids would be buried, but eventually, Violet and Liam were buried at a cemetery in Altadena where generations of Kinley's family had been buried. They'd selected a lovely niche in a gorgeous mausoleum because Bob didn't want the kids out in the elements. He wanted them in a building, protected. They buried Violet and Liam together, in the same white coffin with white satin lining, and slipped them into that lovely niche with a bench next to it where Bob and Linda went on a weekly basis to bring flowers and talk to the kids.

It took all day and into the night for everyone to catch up on what had gone on in the years since Kinley's departure. After Bob and Linda had spoken of the aftermath, Kinley spoke of why she'd gone and what she'd done. There wasn't a lot to tell and, frankly, Kinley felt worse and worse about what she'd put her parents through. After the sun went down and her mother made them something to eat, Kinley sat on the couch, holding her dad's hand while her mother moved around the kitchen making tea.

When it was just Kinley and Bob, the mood turned deep and poignant.

"I just don't know what to say, Dad," she finally said, unable to look the man in the eye. "You went through so much and I am so, so sorry. I should have never... God, even as I started to say that, I know that if I had it to do over again, I would have done the same thing. It was like my mind just shut down. Like I ceased to become Kinley. I wasn't 'me'. Honestly, I don't even remember driving or doing anything until I got up to Wyoming. That's the first time I remember anything at all."

Bob patted her hand. A big man, originally from Texas, he was exceptionally wise. "Your mind just couldn't handle what happened," he said. "Nobody blamed you, Kinley. I want to make that perfectly clear. Nobody blamed you for anything. You didn't know what you were doing."

Kinley was starting to tear up. "I did, but I didn't," she

said. "It took me a long time to remember Gene and Paul coming to the house and telling me what had happened. Paul was crying and Gene could hardly hold it together and when they told me, I didn't even comprehend it. They had to tell me twice more before I began to realize what they were saying."

Bob grunted in sorry, reliving the moment Kinley's colleagues came to tell her that her family had been killed. "I wish they hadn't told you everything," he said. "They told me what they'd said. They didn't hold back. Maybe if they'd been gentler about it, you wouldn't have... well, it doesn't matter now. It's done and you're back. That's all I care about."

Kinley squeezed his hand. "I came back because I needed to come back," she said. "Dad, I'm still not sure I can ever live here again, though. Even coming back here is making me feel sick and anxious. So many memories. But I had to come back to apologize for running out and leaving you and Mom to deal with everything. I had to come back to tell you I'm alive and I'm trying to get on with my life."

"Working in a restaurant?"

She smiled weakly. "It's *my* restaurant," she said. "It's the most popular restaurant in Riverton, Wyoming. It's... it's what I need, Pop. Does that make sense?"

Pop. She'd called him that since she'd been a kid because that was what he'd called his own father, but she intermingled it with 'Dad' and 'Father' and even Bob on occasion. The sassy teenaged Kinley had gone through a phase calling her father Bob because of the reaction he'd give her when she did it. Mostly, he'd yell at her and she would laugh, so he stopped yelling, she stopped laughing, and she eventually forgot about it.

God, he missed that.

He'd missed *her*.

"It makes a whole lot of sense," he said. "We just want you to be happy, Kin. You know that. If it's here or in Wyoming, that's your choice. But I have to say that seeing you again... I can die happy now. I needed to see my girl once more."

Kinley lay her head on his shoulder, wiping at the silent tears that ran down her face. "And I needed to see you," she whispered. "I guess I just needed forgiveness. I needed to tell you how sorry I am for what I did, for the burden on you and Mom. Just know that I never meant to be malicious or cruel. It's like I said... I just lost my mind. I couldn't deal with what happened. I just... shut down."

"I know, honey," Bob said, kissing the top her head. "And there's nothing to forgive. I'm just sorry you had to go through it all. No one should have to suffer what you suffered. It was inhuman. I have to admit that I had a lot of bad thoughts for a while there... you know... thoughts of evening the score. Taking out the guys who did that to the kids and Tom. For a long time I felt like I had to do... *something*."

Kinley experienced a good deal of sorrow for the grandfather who had felt so helpless. "Vigilante stuff?"

"Kind of."

She couldn't blame him. "I think in a situation like

that, any sane person would," she said. "You want to hurt those who have so needlessly hurt you. But me... I couldn't even think that clearly. I could only think about what it had done to *me* and nothing beyond that."

"I can still go take 'em out if you want."

She laughed softly. "Karma will get them," she said. "I really have to believe that. Karma will get them in the end. The universe has a way of righting wrongs like that."

"Let's hope so," Bob said. "I can't say I've ever hoped for death for anyone, but in this case... I still do. I freely admit it."

Kinley curled up on the couch next to him, head on his shoulder, her hand in his. She felt such peace and contentment, her dad with whom she'd always felt safe. She was a grown woman, but he was still trying to take care of her, still trying to take care of her kids. She couldn't seem to stop the tears, not even when her mother brought in a tray with tea and those Pepperidge Farm cookies that her dad liked so much. She tried to pick one up but he snatched it out of her hand like he always did and they laughed. That was so typically her dad.

But he still wouldn't let her have the cookie.

"So what's this I hear about a new boyfriend?" Bob finally said, mouth full of the prized treat. "Ethan says you've got a man up there in the wilds."

Kinley shot her brother an unhappy look, unable to keep the displeased expression off her face. But she quickly relented to the question. "Well, that's a story," she said, taking the cup of tea her mother handed her. "I met him when I was working in a run-down restaurant on the highway up in Wyoming. He was on duty and..."

Bob cut her off. "Law enforcement?"

"Yes," Kinley said, continuing. "He's a sheriff's deputy. His dad is the county sheriff, in fact. Anyway, he came in for lunch and the place ended up getting held up. The robbers were going to kill him, but I managed to get a hold of the shotgun behind the counter and capped two of them before they could pull the trigger. I guess I saved his life and in return, he saved mine."

Bob and Linda were looking at her with horror. "Wow," Bob said. "No kidding?"

"No kidding."

"But how did he save yours?"

She forced a smile. "I'm here, aren't I?" she said. "He's helped me work through a lot of stuff. He helped me realize that running wasn't going to do any good. I had to face my fears. I had to find the Kinley I was before everything happened. So... here I am."

Bob sighed heavily, looking at his wife, who was both distressed and grateful. "Then I owe him my thanks," he said, looking back to his daughter. "Sounds like a hell of a guy."

"He is," Kinley said. "Very understanding, very patient. I... I haven't been very nice to him, I'll admit it. But I'm going to change that. I love him. You may as well know that."

Both Bob and Linda smiled. "That's such good news," Bob said. "Thank God, that's good news."

"Where is he?" Linda asked. "Did he stay in Wyoming?"

Kinley shook her head. "He followed me out here," she said. "He just didn't want to intrude on our reunion. He said I had to do this alone."

"Smart man," Bob said. "But if he's out here, I'd like to meet him."

"You will," Kinley said. "I want to visit the kids and I asked him to do go with me. Do you mind?"

Bob shook his head. "Not at all," he said. "Why not invite him over for breakfast and we'll go up to the mausoleum afterwards?"

Kinley sighed faintly, looking at the window to see that it was dark outside. "It's not open now, is it?"

"No, honey. They open in the morning but close around four."

Kinley had to accept that even though now that she was home, the pull to see her children was very strong. The maternal instinct was in overdrive. Knowing that her father had spent time with the children after their death gave her such comfort, but in that comfort was also a mother's curiosity and a mother's pain. She began to tear up again, fearful to ask questions that her heart and soul wanted answers to.

"Pop?" she asked softly, looking at her teacup.

"What?"

"The kids... they weren't... it was instant, wasn't it?"

"Yes."

"Were they torn up?"

Bob watched her tears falling onto her chest, her arm, as she stared down at her teacup. "How much do you want to know?" he asked quietly.

"I can't listen," Linda said, standing up and heading for the kitchen. "I'm sorry, I just can't."

Kinley waited until her mother was out of the room before speaking again. "It was bad, wasn't it?" she asked, her voice tight.

Bob sighed heavily and set his teacup down. "It was bad," he said. "But take comfort in the fact that they never felt a thing. Not a damn thing. Okay?"

"Do you have the autopsy reports?"

Bob nodded in resignation. "I do."

"Please let me see them."

"Kin..."

"*Please*, Dad. I want to know everything. I... I have to."

Bob looked to Ethan for guidance. He was so torn. But Ethan, who had read the reports, nodded once. It was Kinley's right. They'd hoped to spare her, but the mother in her was asking. She wanted to know what happened to her babies.

The moment had come for her to finally face it.

After Kinley read the reports, she cried all night.

THIRTEEN

"THE GUY IS part of an offshoot gang in Echo Park," Reed was saying. "When Kinley told me she was coming out here, I spent all night researching the gangs and records, researching the guys who did that to her family. I'm serious about this, Trace."

Sitting on the side yard of a gorgeous vintage Mission Revival-style home in Pasadena, one built by a railroad magnate back in the day and had been turned into a popular bed and breakfast and micro-wedding venue, Reed had just outlined his plans to Trace Rocklin. His friend, his comrade, even his accomplice.

The one and only Eliminator.

"And payback's a bitch?" Trace said quietly.

Reed simply shrugged and took a swig of his beer from some microbrewery in Pasadena. It was good, but it smelled and tasted too much like oranges for him. Still, he was on his third bottle, chatting it up with Trace while

Trace's lovely wife, Kiki, chased around a curly-haired toddler. When the kid ran up to his dad and demanded a taste of his beer and Trace pretended he had no idea what the child was asking for, Reed had to turn his head away, laughing because Trace's wife was pissed off about it. Kiki swung the baby into her arms and took him into the house as Trace continued to pretend he had no idea what the child was crying about. When he looked at Reed and their gazes met, both men broke down into snorts.

"She's right, you know," Reed said. "You don't want to give a baby beer."

Trace shrugged, taking a drink of his beer. "You know what he does?" he said. "He puts the top of the bottle in his mouth and nothing more. He thinks he's drinking beer, but he's not. Just the fumes. Can I help it if he wants to be just like me?"

Reed continued to chuckle, shaking his head. "We all want to be just like you," he said, sobering. "Even me. Even for just a weekend."

Trace sobered as well as the reason for Reed's visit became the focus again. Trace had just listened to an hour's worth of why Reed was here and what he intended to do while he was out here, which sounded more like a Hollywood movie plot. Not that Reed couldn't pull it off, but it was ambitious at best.

A reckoning aways was.

And it was damn serious.

"I get why you want to do this," Trace said quietly. "Believe me, I get it. But it's not like we're in the Ukraine or Turkey or Syria. What you want to do, here in America, could have some... repercussions."

Reed shook his head. "With whom?" he said, keeping his voice down because he didn't want Trace's wife to hear their conversation. "Local law enforcement? I can pull this off in such a way that they'll never be able to trace anything to me. I'll make it look like another gang or just a random attack. Look, the guy who killed Kinley's family is in jail and he'll fucking rot there, but the guy she put away – the one who put the hit out on her – got out six months ago. Good behavior or some shit like that. He's the one, Trace. It started with him."

"And it's going to end with him?"

"Something like that," Reed muttered. Taking a long, pensive breath, he sank back in the patio chair. "Her whole family, man. He ordered a hit on her whole family. How'd you feel if someone took out Austin and Kiki?"

Trace lifted his eyebrows. "I think you know how I'd feel."

"That's how *I* feel," Reed said. "Kinley... she's strong and noble. She didn't deserve what happened to her. I spent more than twenty years using my training to accomplish some of the most difficult missions in the world. I'm retired now, but that agent in me hasn't died. But you know what scares me? That Kinley resurfaces and it becomes public knowledge, and the asshole who ordered the hit on her family goes after her again. And I'm not going to live with the fear of losing her. I lost one woman I loved. I'm not doing it again, not if I can do something about it."

"I feel you, brother."

Reed felt validated, letting himself experience the anger and fear he would have never shown Kinley, not when she was already so fragile. But when she told him that she was coming home to face her past, he knew he just couldn't stand by and let her enter the lion's den again. Those same people who had ordered the hit on her family were still out there.

Reed couldn't stand by and do nothing.

He'd made the decision.

"She saved my life once," he said after a moment. "I need to repay that favor."

Trace pondered that, watching a hummingbird on a nearby vine go from flower to flower. "When do you want to do it?"

Reed drained the rest of his beer, smacking his lips. "It has to be while I'm out here and I don't know how long that's going to be, so I'm going to drive over to Echo Park tomorrow," he said. "I have an address. I need to see the layout."

"And then what?"

"And then I'll decide what needs to be done."

"You sure you want to do this?"

"If we were talking about Kiki, how sure would you be?"

Trace was still looking at the vine and the humming-bird. He didn't say anything right away. But after a few moments, he turned his head toward the house where Kiki was in the kitchen window, washing off the hands of her son, who was more interested in playing in the water.

"Kiki?" he called. "Honey?"

Kiki heard him and reached across the sink to open the window. "What?"

"Do you care if I go with Reed to visit a mutual friend over the weekend?" he said. "Just guy stuff. Are you okay with that?"

"Sure," she said. "Do you want to take the little monster with you? He's a guy. He can do guy stuff."

He grinned. "Can I leave him here?"

"Coward."

"Damn right."

Kiki laughed and closed the window. Reed hadn't said a word the entire time and even now looked to Trace for an explanation as to what had just happened. Trace took another drink of his beer before replying.

"We'll hang out here a little while longer and then get going," he said.

"*We?*" Reed said. "Trace, I didn't ask you to go with me."

"Tough shit. I'm going."

Reed wasn't necessarily happy with that. "This is my thing," he said quietly. "While I appreciate that you want to help, I don't want you involved."

Trace looked at him, then. "Like I said – tough shit," he said. "You're not going without me, Reed. *Angelus Destruens.*"

Reed looked at him, hearing something he hadn't heard in years come out of Trace's mouth. He knew what it meant. Anyone part of the Unholy Angels knew what it meant. It was their battle cry and to hear it coming from Trace almost brought tears to his eyes. It meant he wasn't alone, not ever, no matter where life took him and what he needed to accomplish, his brothers were always there.

Angelues Destruens.

Destroying Angels.

Maybe a little help for what he intended to do wasn't a bad thing.

"Okay," he whispered reluctantly. "I get it."

"You're not going to fight me on it?"

"Would it do any good?"

"Nope."

An hour later, Trace kissed his wife and fussy son goodbye and headed out with Reed. Trace told Kiki that they were heading out to Santa Monica and he'd talk to her tomorrow, but the truth was that they were heading out to buy some pre-paid burner phones and do some reconnaissance.

They had plans to make.

FOURTEEN

KINLEY COULDN'T EAT breakfast that morning.

After getting zero sleep because of the autopsy reports, her stomach was in knots as day broke over the San Gabriel Mountains. Standing in her folks' backyard with a cup of coffee in-hand, she gazed up at the purple mountains just as the sun came over the eastern horizon. It was cool and crisp outside, a fresh day just waiting to be lived. Being an alumni of Pasadena High School, the moment reminded her of the words to the school's alma mater.

Sturdy as the mountains,
Lovely as the dawn.
Hail, Pasadena
Fearless and strong.

When she'd been a student at the high school built sometime during the 1950's, an enormous campus that spread out over several acres, she could have never imagined what life had in store for her. The sky was the limit for Kinley Connors. She'd done everything in high school – marching band, cheerleading, French Club, Debate Team. You name it, she'd done it. She even participated in the spring musicals that were performed in the big auditorium that smelled like dust and old wood. Her senior year, she'd been Annie in "Annie Get Your Gun." She'd been perfect in rehearsals but on opening night, she'd had a panic attack that had forever killed her desire to be an actress. Instead, she went to college and then into law enforcement.

Maybe being an actress would have been better.

Being in law enforcement had only brought her trouble.

Sipping on her coffee, she waited until seven in the morning to call Reed, but he didn't pick up. She tried him again before she got dressed an hour later and simply left a message. She'd had hopes that he might have come to breakfast and met her parents, but breakfast came and went with no return call from Reed. Kinley was disappointed but that emotion quickly faded at the prospect of seeing her kids today.

The reason behind her inability to eat.

The autopsy report was back in her dad's safe, but the words were indelibly imprinted on her brain. So was the diagram of each body. Violet had tried to protect herself. Liam never knew what hit him. Tom had gotten it first, so he was already gone when the car crashed into a light post and the gang members jumped out of their car and unloaded clips into her vehicle. Kinley was sorry she'd read the reports, but not sorry she read the reports. Her emotions were all over the place. To her, it underscored what a horrific act of cowardice it was. An act of unreasonable destruction. But after reading it, and after no sleep, she was ready to see her kids.

She had a lot to say to them.

"Good morning," Bob said as he came into the kitchen where Kinley was pouring the last of the coffee into her cup. "How'd you sleep?"

Kinley began to make another pot for her dad. "I didn't."

He grunted. "I knew I shouldn't have given you those reports."

She looked at him. "No, I'm glad you did," she said. "My inability to sleep isn't your fault. I needed to read the reports, Dad. It gives me a better idea of what actually happened. Oddly, I do have some peace."

Bob nudged her out of the way and finished making the coffee. "Well, as long as you're satisfied with it," he said. "I haven't read them since I saw them the first time. I have to say that they gave me nightmares."

Kinley leaned against the counter, watching him pour in the water. "I thought a lot about it last night," she said. "You have to understand this is something I haven't really let myself think long and hard about. Ignoring it seemed to be the only way to keep my sanity, but I was ready to read those reports. Ready to face it. Sure, it was upsetting, but I feel like I've accomplished something by getting through them."

Bob looked at her. "Accomplished what?"

She shrugged. "Understanding, mostly," she said, taking a sip of coffee. "Vi and Liam are gone. I've accepted that. But now I'm in the 'how' phase. I just needed to understand 'how.' Now, I know."

"Now you do."

"Can I ask you a question?"

"Sure."

"Did you see them together in the casket?"

Bob paused, watching the coffee trickle into the pot. "I did," he said quietly. "I brought the clothes to the funeral home. Liam wore the suit you bought him for Easter that year. Vi wore her Easter dress, too."

"And Tom?"

"His parents took care of that," he said. "He wore a suit."

"Was the service for all three of them?"

"It was. We thought that was best."

Kinley could see that the questions were distressing him. "Sorry, Dad," she said, putting a hand on his arm. "I just want to know one more thing and I'll stop asking."

He shook his head. "You don't have to stop asking," he said. "You weren't there and you want to know. I get it."

"I know that, but I also know that it's upsetting to you to remember that stuff," she said. "But... just tell me one more thing."

"What?"

"How... how were the kids positioned in the casket? In my mind's eye, I just want to see them."

"Facing each other," Bob said, remembering that particularly horrible vision right before the funeral directors closed the casket. "Vi was kind of holding Liam against her. An embrace. And there was a white baby blanket that Tom's mother made that was tucked in around them."

Kinley nodded, thinking of her children in their eternal embrace. The tears started to come before she could stop them. "Thanks for telling me," she said, quickly wiping them away. "Can we go to the cemetery now? Is it open?"

Bob glanced at the clock. "It opens at nine," he said. "Get your stuff and we'll head up."

Kinley headed back to her old bedroom to grab her purse. She checked her cell phone one last time only to see that there were no calls. Wherever Reed was, he was either busy or maybe even still asleep. Honestly, maybe she really wasn't too disappointed that he wasn't coming because she wanted to see her kids alone for the first time. Alone so she could tell them everything she needed to tell them, just her and Vi and Liam. Just the three of them. She'd go see Tom at some point, too, but right now, it was just about the kids.

She was ready to face them and apologize.

It was time.

FIFTEEN

HIS NAME WAS Cesar Alvarez Rodriquez.

His life could be measured in hours.

West of Dodger Stadium and northeast of downtown Los Angeles, Echo Park was an older community with long established Southern California history. It had been founded in 1892 as a community called Edendale and had been the center of filmmaking long before Hollywood came into existence. There had been old-timey studios built in the city and such notable film stars as Fatty Arbuckle, Gloria Swanson, Mabel Normand and more had worked at those studios back in the day. A very old Mack Sennett sound stage from 1909 still existed, now part of a storage facility.

Echo Park had proud and old roots.

But it wasn't the best of neighborhoods these days. Graffiti ruled the streets and fortified homes were wedged into the hillsides like mini-castles, made strong against the violence that so often plagued the town. Almost all of the homes and apartment buildings in the city were heavily fortified, something Reed and Trace had been forced to deal with. They had an address for Cesar, aka Mickey Mouse, and his family, but it was a home that had a big fence around it and big dogs in the yard. That meant that anything Trace and Reed did would have to be done outside the home.

And they had a plan.

Reed had actually found out quite a bit about the man who had ordered the death of Kinley's family. Cesar and his two brothers, Alonzo and Jose, had fallen out with the gang they'd been part of after the killing of Kinley's family. Even though Trace knew a guy who worked for the Los Angeles Police Department, he didn't want to tip him off by asking about the Echo Park gangs, so the information they came up with was searchable in the web and mutual aid databases. They'd gotten it off of a cheap laptop they'd bought and then smashed and tossed into the ocean off of Santa Monica so it couldn't be traced. But their research had produced enough to tell them that Mickey Mouse had been kicked out of his gang and started another one called Grafton EP. From what Reed and Trace could tell, it wasn't a big gang and not very important.

And that would work to Reed and Trace's advantage, too.

No allies or fellow gang members to create barriers.

In fact, Reed and Trace had been at it for two straight days. Reed hadn't even spoken to Kinley because of it. She had called him, several times, and he didn't pick up the phone because he didn't want his cell phone to triangulate off of cell towers in Echo Park. He didn't want it proven that he was anywhere near Echo Park should it ever come up. So, he ignored her calls, as difficult as it was, because he knew she wanted him to meet her parents and go to the cemetery with her. But this, in his opinion, was more important.

He had a little business to take care of first.

His mission with Trace had started when they'd stolen a car from Pico Rivera, one with Sonora plates, and drove it into Los Angeles. They wore baseball caps and false facial hair that they'd purchased at a costume store, trying to disguise themselves as much as they were able. Given Trace had blond hair, he kept it covered up and the facial hair he had on him was dark. Everyone had security cameras these days so even if they showed up on someone's feed, they were disguised as much as they could be.

Nothing to trace them.

As the second night rolled around, they were sitting at the bottom of the hill on the street that Cesar and his family lived. The car they had was so beat up and rusted that it fit in perfectly with the surrounding vehicles. Using binoculars, they were able to watch the house, the comings and goings, and they identified Cesar early on. They also identified his car.

And that was their target.

"Well?" Trace said, lowering the binoculars. "He's

been out twice today, bringing back cases of beer every time. Looks like the guy is going to have a party."

Reed, slumped in the driver's seat, nodded. "Yeah," he said. "If we could ignite the car at the house, the collateral damage would be substantial."

"Is that what you want to do?"

Reed looked at him. "Possibly," he said quietly. "If I take out his brothers, too, then consider it payback for the two little kids they killed. Do you have enough ammonium nitrate to blow the car?"

Trace nodded. "That's one of the advantages of working for a construction company that does demolition from time to time," he said. "We keep a tight record of the stuff, but I'm the one who keeps the records, so my dad will never know. It comes in big bags and I just happen to have a bag."

"It's a controlled substance."

"And we've got a license," Trace said, looking at him. "I've got the stuff and a detonator that can't be traced, either. Do you want to do this or not?"

"I do."

"We can blow the car or we can use firearms."

Reed shrugged. "They've been coming in and out of the house enough that we can use the firearms," he said. "That may be the quieter way to go. If we blow up half the block, it'll trigger much more of an investigation. And they may find residue and realize it was ammonium nitrate. That'll open up a can of worms because they can trace it to manufacturers and customer lists."

Trace shrugged. "Whatever you want to do," he said. "You want me to take the shot?"

Reed's gaze moved back to the home up the hill. "This is where I say I need to do this because it's my problem," he said. "But we both know you're a better marksman than I am."

"So we do a drive-by?"

"That's what happens in these neighborhoods, you know. They cops will investigate but they'll attribute it to a rival gang."

"That's better than blowing up a car, I suppose," Trace said. "There aren't many gangs out there who plant car bombs with construction-grade ammonium nitrate."

"True," Reed said. "Then we wait for them to come back out again and drive by."

"I'm ready."

They had several guns, including one they'd found under the seat of the car they'd stolen. Trace hadn't fired it yet, but he could shoot any gun, any time, so he planned on using it because it was the perfect weapon. Probably an illegal gun, kept in a car that probably still hadn't been registered in the United States yet.

There was no way this was coming back on them.

Reaching under the seat with his gloved hands, he pulled the gun out. It was a 9mm Glock in perfect condition, an elegant weapon meant to do a lot of damage. Trace inspected it carefully as Reed kept watch on the house up the hill. The conversation fell silent for few moments while Trace checked the clip, the bullets, and the moving components of the gun.

"Just like old times," he muttered, glancing at Reed and watching the man smile. "I miss those days, to tell you the truth. Just not enough to get back into the game."

Reed nodded in agreement. "I like where I am," he said. "Quiet life for the most part, back home where my parents live. It's where I belong."

"Does Kinley know about your work with the CIA?"

Reed shrugged. "I told her I was in the Marines and also worked with the CIA, so she knows in a general sense," he said. "I've never gone into detail. She doesn't need to know that part of it."

"Like the part we're doing now."

"Exactly."

"You're not going to tell her about this?'

Reed shook his head. "No," he said quietly. "Why would I? What purpose would it serve?"

Trace slapped the clip back into the gun. "Maybe give her a sense of closure," he said. "Like you said, the woman lost her whole family. If it was me, I'd sure like to know that those responsible had paid for it in blood and who I had to thank for it."

Reed looked at him. "You and me think alike, but I'm not sure she thinks that way," he said. "It may be a little much for her to take. I think it's better just to let it lie."

Reed's phone began to ring again and both men looked down. They could see who was calling. "She's been calling you for two days," Trace said quietly. "What are you going to tell her? You followed her out here for moral support while she faced her past, but then you disappear? How are you going to deal with that?"

Reed watched it go to voicemail again. "I can't risk a cell tower around here picking up the call if I answer it," he said. "I'll just have to tell her that we went on a drinking binge or something. Or my phone malfunctioned."

"Then you should just turn it off."

Reed nodded reluctantly, picked up his phone, and turned off the power. "I'll call her tomorrow regardless of what happens tonight," he said. "She's going to start to worry if she can't get a hold of me and then it'll be harder to explain me dropping off the face of the earth."

That was the truth. Trace could see that Reed was sweating it, but he didn't want to move from the stakeout and he didn't want to risk calling her. They went back to sitting in silence, watching the house as the sun began to set. People began arriving around dinner time, bringing more beer and presents. A birthday party. There were even kids around, but that didn't deter either of them. Not when Mickey Mouse didn't give a damn about Kinley's kids.

Then, as the streetlights went on, something happened.

Cesar and a couple of other guys came out to the Chevy Impala parked on the street and climbed in. The headlights went on and they pulled away, heading down the hill as Reed and Trace hit the deck so they wouldn't be seen. The car passed them by and they sat up, watching it go to the end of the street and take a right turn.

Reed fired up the old Ford Crown Victoria and made a U-turn, heading off quickly after Cesar and his friends. Once they made the right turn, they were nearing Glendale Boulevard but Cesar's car wasn't difficult to spot because it was bright blue with chrome rims. Reed and Trace followed him at a distance to a liquor store a few miles away and parked down the street, watching him and his friends go in and then come out several minutes later bearing another case of beer.

When the Chevy made a U-turn to go back the way it came, Reed and Trace didn't want to be seen again so they quickly turned up another street, one that intersected with a street that joined with the street that Cesar's home was situated on. In fact, they realized that they could cut Cesar off as he returned home and that's exactly what they intended to do.

On a dark, warm Los Angeles night, Reed and Trace lay in wait for Cesar's car to come down the street and when they saw him coming, Reed gunned the car so that it abruptly blocked the intersection. Cesar had to slam on his breaks to avoid hitting them, but before he could yell at them or drive around them, Trace and Reed bailed out and opened fire on the car.

Twenty-four bullets from Trace's high-capacity clip emptied into Cesar's car along with seventeen bullets from Reed's weapon. Cesar and his friends were dead in short order and once the firing stopped, dogs in the area were barking wildly. Smoke filled the air. But Cesar was wiped out and that was all Reed was concerned with. He didn't even stop to check the bodies because he could see that someone's brains had been blown out all over the inside of the car. There was no need. He and Trace bailed back into their car and sped off, back toward Los Angeles where they would return the car where they found it. An illegal gun, a car with Sonoran plates, and no tags.

Let the cops sort it out.

The Destroying Angels lived up to their name that night.

SIXTEEN

HE WASN'T PICKING up his phone.

Kinley was trying not to stress out about Reed's disappearance, but after two days of not hearing from him, she was starting to wonder if he'd decided he didn't want any part of this. Not that she blamed him, but she was back to feeling the anxiety she'd felt when she'd flown out to L.A. alone, afraid she was never going to see him again.

She tried not to let it bother her.

On the evening of the second day, she decided to simply stop calling him. He had her number and knew where to find her. In one of her recent messages, she mentioned that she was going back to the cemetery in the morning to see the kids and she told him where it was. That way, he could join her if he wanted to.

But she wasn't holding her breath.

Staying at her parents' house, sleeping in her old room, had been an experience that she hadn't counted on. When she'd moved out all those years ago, her parents had converted it into a guest room, so she was essentially sleeping on her childhood bed that her mother had painted and put a new bedspread on. The first night hadn't been so great, but the second night had been better. It had been cathartic to sleep in that room, taking her back to a time in her life where she'd been carefree and young, and the simple things that made her happy. She was finally able to breathe in a safe space and that, probably more than anything, helped her mental state.

She was home.

She was safe.

Everything was going to be all right.

On the morning of the third day, she woke up to her mother making pancakes and bacon and eggs, and she sat next to her dad at the breakfast bar and stuffed herself. It was a morning that was peaceful and normal, with her dad hogging the bacon and her mother picking on him because he shouldn't be eating it. It had been good to hear that again. She laughed at her dad, who would shove bacon in his mouth when her mother wasn't looking and then blame Kinley for eating all of the bacon. She'd missed these moments so much. Healing moments that healed the bullet wounds that had damaged her soul.

But still, no Reed.

Honestly, she was so puzzled about him that she just didn't know what to think – and it was difficult not to think about it, although she was trying. After breakfast, she showered and got dressed, preparing to go up to the cemetery again because her dad had called Tom's parents the night before and told them that Kinley had returned. They wanted to see her, so Bob told them to meet her up at the cemetery in the morning. In cropped white pants, a cute shirt, and her long hair pulled into a ponytail, Kinley climbed into the back seat of her father's truck, with Bob and Linda in the front seat, as they headed up to Altadena to visit Vi and Liam.

It was the second time in two days that Kinley would visit her kids, but she had a lot to make up for. The day before, on her first visit, she'd spent six hours sitting next to their crypt, saying everything she wanted to say, sobbing in a way she hadn't sobbed before. It was a cry of profound loss, of grief, and of healing. It had been six hours of hysterics. Bob and Linda had brought her up to the mausoleum, but they'd stayed away while she grieved alone. The truth was that they'd stood outside the mausoleum entrance and even from that distance, they had heard her crying. Bob had wanted to go in and comfort her, but Linda made him stay outside.

This was Kinley's moment.

There wasn't much her father could do, anyway.

Therefore, Bob kept looking at her in the rearview mirror as they headed up Lake Avenue in Pasadena. Kinley had her sunglasses on, watching the familiar sights roll by, but she knew her dad was watching her. It was becoming ridiculous.

"Dad," she muttered. "*Stop.*"

Bob glanced at her. "Stop what?"

"I'm not going to collapse," she said. "I'm okay today. Everything is going to be fine. Stop looking at me like I'm going to implode."

Bob cleared his throat as he focused on the road ahead. "I'm not," he said. "But Ed and Jeanie are going to be there today. I worry... well, I worry how you're going to feel about that."

Kinley shrugged, watching a particularly old block of buildings go by. She pointed. "Mom, remember the toy store that used to be there?" she said. "They had kids' birthday parties there in a creepy back room that smelled like mildew. I had a party there one year. Remember?"

Linda nodded. "You sure did," she said. "You got a pretty doll from your grandmother, but you wanted a car that had batteries in it. You told your grandmother to trade the doll in for it."

Kinley started laughing. "And she did," she said. "I remember that."

"She sure did," Linda said with regret. "She should have smacked you one."

Kinley's laughter continued. "Those were the days," she said. "Making Grandma bend to my will. She was such a pushover."

Linda grinned. "She was," she agreed. "She was for both you and Ethan. But you made up for it by naming your daughter after her. She would have loved that."

Kinley nodded. "She would have, totally," she said. Her dad pulled to a stoplight, preparing to make the turn onto the street where the cemetery was located. "In answer to your question, Dad, I don't know how I'm going to feel about seeing Ed and Jeanie. I'm probably going to cry. But I do want to see them."

Bob nodded, making the turn onto a wide, residential street that would connect to a more commercial area and the cemetery.

"Just so you know, they took Tom's death hard," he said. "He was their only son, so they took it really hard. He's buried near their house and Ed told me they visit his grave several times a week. They just wanted him close to them."

"I don't blame them," Kinley said. "But I like that Vi and Liam are with Grandma Violet and Grandpa William, and Great-Grandma Ella and Great-Grandpa Harvey, and the twenty other relatives we have at Mountain View. They're well-protected and watched over."

"That's the way I see it," Bob said. "And when your mom and I pass on, we bought the crypt right next to them, so we'll be with them, too."

That thought had tears stinging Kinley's eyes. "I love that you did that, Dad," she said, reaching over to pat his shoulder. "You have no idea how much comfort that gives me."

"There's space for you, too, someday."

"And I'll take you up on that."

"Any thought to moving back here, Kin?" Linda said, looking back at her.

"Linda..." Bob hissed, shaking his head.

Kinley took her hand off her dad's shoulder. "I'm not

sure yet," she said softly. "I've made a life for myself away from this and as much as I love being here with you, the memories of grief and sadness are still really heavy. This whole place just feels sad and heavy to me, so I'm not sure I'm ready to live like that. In Riverton, there's no grief or sadness. It's fresh, without the memories. I'm not sure I can explain it any better than that."

"You don't have to," Bob said. "We understand even though your mom pretends she doesn't."

"That's not fair, Bob," Linda said, frowning. "I was just asking a question."

"Stop asking. She'll tell you when she's ready."

Kinley sat forward, putting her hand between her parents to block their view of one another. "Stop arguing," she said, grinning. "I love you both, but knock it off. This is a happy day, okay? I intend to be happier today than yesterday. I'll hug Ed and Jeanie, and talk to Vi and Liam, and I'm going to be joyful. Okay?"

Both of her parents, miffed at one another, simply nodded. Still grinning, Kinley sat back in the seat until her father pulled into the mausoleum parking lot.

Then, those feelings of grief and sadness began to overwhelm her again.

As soon as Bob turned off the car, Kinley bailed out and took off toward the entrance to the mausoleum. Bob and Linda were barely out of the car when Kinley was halfway to the door. That had Bob holding his wife back because he suspected Kinley needed some alone time with her kids again. Six hours of crying the day before had only been the start of it. He looked at his wife sadly, indicating for her to get back into the truck, and she did. A glance around the parking lot showed that Ed and Jeanie Berrington weren't there yet, so Bob decided to wait for them and give his daughter some space. Turning on the local news radio, he and Linda settled down for the wait.

The innards of the mausoleum were cold and beautiful. Her children were waiting and Kinley wanted to get to them, so she slipped inside the building and headed for the far end of the main wing. It really was a gorgeous building with stunning stained glass, but there was an eeriness about it. So many dead in one place, in one building, all of them sleeping peacefully.

Just like her kids.

As soon as she turned the corner, she ended up in a two-storied room with a vaulted ceiling that had the feel of the Sistine Chapel. As she headed toward the far end, she could see someone down there. She was a little disappointed because she'd hoped to be alone for a few minutes to say hello to her children, but the closer she came, the more she realized that she recognized the figure. When he stood up from the bench he'd been sitting on, Kinley started to run.

It was Reed.

"Oh, my God," she said, throwing herself into his open arms as he lifted her up. "You came!"

Reed held her tightly. "Of course I came," he said. "I wouldn't miss an invitation like this. In fact, I just introduced myself to Violet and Liam. I looked around for Tom but I didn't see him."

Kinley relaxed her grip on him and he put her on her feet. "He's not here," she said. "His parents wanted him buried closer to their house."

"Ah," he said in understanding. He looked at her for a moment before bending down to kiss her and give her another hug. "I've missed you. Are you okay? How has the visit been?"

Kinley kissed him again because she was so happy to see him. "It's been better than I hoped," she said. She paused before continuing. "I've been calling you for two days. Did you get my messages?"

"I did."

"I thought you might have gone back home without me."

Reed rolled his eyes. Then he put his hand over his face as if this was a subject he didn't want to talk about, and the truth was that he didn't, but he and Trace had come up with a good story. At least, he hoped so.

He was going to give it a shot.

"I would *not* have gone home without you, I promise," he said. "But.. well, you're not going to believe this, but I went to visit a buddy of mine that I used to work with at the CIA. The one I told you about."

"The guy that lives in Pasadena?"

"Exactly," he said. "Him. His name is Trace Rocklin and his wife's name is Kiki. They've got this little terror of a toddler I've had to put up with for two days. Anyway,

I've been with him. I got shit-faced on tequila or something he gave me the first night and I think I spent the next whole day sleeping it off. We were doing shots of this liquor he said was really good, but that stuff made me sick. So damn sick. Do I look like I've lost ten pounds? Because I feel like I've thrown up enough to lose that much weight."

Kinley looked at him, from head to toe. "You look great," she said. "But why didn't you call me and tell me? I could have taken care of you so your friend didn't have to do it."

He jabbed a finger at her. "*That's* why," he said. "Because if I told you I wasn't well, you would have dropped everything to come to me and I wasn't going to let you do it. This is your trip, honey. Not mine. I didn't want to distract you from the reason you were here in the first place."

She frowned. "That wouldn't have distracted me," she said. "Okay, maybe a little, but are you sure you're okay? Maybe you do look a little pale."

He waved her off. "I'm fine," he said. "I told Trace that he'd better be on call because you might not believe that I've spent two days recovering from a drinking binge and he would have to explain it to you. Christ, I could handle something like that in college, but I'm old now. Old and fragile. It just made me sick and miserable and the whole time, Trace has got this screaming kid who wanted to put toy dinosaurs on my head as I was laying there, defenseless."

Kinley grinned. "I would have paid money to see that."

"Another reason why I didn't call you, you mean woman."

Kinley laughed. More importantly, she bought his excuse. She had no reason not to. She gave him another hug, this time in sympathy, before they turned, with their arms around one another, to the crypt with Violet and Liam's name on it. It was right there in front of them, the marble warming in the early morning light.

Violet Jean Connors-Berrington
Liam Robert Connors-Berrington
Sleep well, little angels, until we meet again.

"This is a nice place," Reed said softly, looking at the delicate face of the crypt. "And a gorgeous building."

Kinley had her head on his chest as she looked at the crypt, reaching out to gently touch it. "It's perfect," she said, struggling against the grief that was threatening to come back in a tidal wave. "My dad picked it. I have several relatives buried around here, and my parents bought the crypt right next to the kids because he wanted to watch over them. Even in death."

"That's really sweet."

"It is," Kinley said. "I didn't realize how much I missed my parents until I got out here and saw them again. It's going to be really hard to go back to Wyoming."

He had a big arm around her. "Honey, you don't have to go back if you don't want to," he said quietly. "*This* is your home. If you wanted to stay, I wouldn't blame you."

She shrugged. "I know," she said. "But like I told my dad, it still feels like sorrow and grief out here. I'm facing up to it, but it still feels... heavy. I don't know if I can live like that, at least not now. Maybe in a few years I'll come back, but right now... I just don't know."

He gave her a squeeze. "It's your decision," he said. "I'll support whatever you want to do."

"But you won't come with me if I move out here, will you?"

He looked at her. "I don't know," he said. "I haven't been asked."

"I'm asking."

His eyes glimmered warmly. "I will follow you anywhere," he said. "But I think you already know that. If you want to come back to California, then I guess I'm coming, too."

She smiled up at him. "That's so sweet," she said. "But your job and your parents are in Wyoming. I hate to take you away from your life there."

"I can always get another job and I have lived away from my parents before."

"You'd get a job out here?"

"I'd lateral over to the sheriff's department, I suppose."

"My dad was an assistant sheriff. I'm sure he could help."

Reed chuckled softly. "Then it's good to have connections."

There didn't seem to be anything more to say. Kinley smiled at him and he kissed her on top of the head as she clung tightly to him, hearing his heartbeat in her right ear, drawing strength from the man. But she put out a free hand, touching the marble face of her children's crypt again, as the tears started to come.

"I'm so glad you're here," she whispered tightly. "I wanted you to meet them. Whenever Vi met someone new, she would always draw them a picture. She would have given you a picture of the sun or something. She liked to draw the sun."

He smiled. "Cute," he said. "You probably had a house full of pictures from her, right?"

"Right," Kinley whispered, closing her eyes as she thought of the reams of paper her daughter went through and how they were literally all over the house. "My parents probably cleaned out my house and just packed up everything. I'll have to ask my dad where everything is."

"Did they drive you up here?"

"Yes," she said. "They should be here any minute."

Reed dropped his arm from her and stepped away. "I haven't met your dad yet," he said. "I don't want him coming in here and finding you in an embrace with a strange man."

Kinley grinned, wiping the tears from her eyes. "He knows about you," she said. "I told him. I'm really eager for you to meet my parents. You'll love my dad. He's a lot like you. Kind of big and strong. Oh... my God, so strong... you know, he told me that he went to the house after they told him what happened and when the medical examiner took the kids away, he followed the truck all the way to the morgue. He stayed with them for two days until they convinced him it was okay to go home and they'd watch out for the kids. That's the kind of man he is, Reed. He wouldn't leave the kids at all."

Reed wasn't smiling anymore. He was shaking his head, in awe of what he'd just heard. "Wow," he finally said. "That's really incredible. Such a good grandpa."

Kinley nodded. "I know," she said. "There's so much more to tell, I don't even know where to start."

He put his hand on her back, gently. "We have plenty of time," he said. "Besides, the story isn't over yet."

"What do you mean?"

"I mean that you're still here, in California," he said. "The visit isn't over. That means your story isn't finished yet."

She nodded. "True," she said. "I put in a call to my old captain. To say he was shocked to hear from me is an understatement. But he wants to meet up with me before I go back to Wyoming. Will you come?"

"If you want me to."

Before Kinley could answer, the sounds of footsteps suddenly filled the corridor and they looked to see a tall, silver-haired man walking towards them. Kinley held up a hand in greeting as he came closer.

"Hey, Dad," she said. "You're just in time. This is Reed McCoy, the guy I told you about. Reed, this is my dad, Bob Connors."

Reed extended a hand to the man who immediately took it. "Nice to meet you," Reed said.

Bob shook his hand firmly, taking a good look at the man who helped return his daughter to him. "You, too," he said. "Kinley's talked so much about you I feel like we're old friends."

Reed smiled. "That's nice to hear," he said. "I hope it's okay for me to come here. I don't want to intrude on anything."

Bob waved him off. "Not at all," he said. "You're very welcome, anytime. But... if I can have a word with my daughter for second?"

Reed started to leave but Bob stopped him, instead pulling Kinley with him. She looked at her father curiously as he pulled her down the corridor with crypts on either side, surrounded by white marble and streams of sunlight from the windows overhead, until they finally came to a stop.

The conversation started.

Reed pretended to inspect the other crypts around the kids, looking at the names and dates, when he was really paying attention to the body language as the Kinley and her father had what looked like a rather serious discussion. It went on for several minutes until Bob eventually left Kinley standing by herself as he went back outside.

Slowly, and seemingly dazed, Kinley made her way over to Reed.

"Hey," he said. "If you'd like me to step out and wait for you outside while your parents come back in, I can. Maybe they want some quiet time with you and the kids without a stranger hanging around."

She was shaking her head before he even finished. "No," she said. "It's nothing like that."

He could tell that she was distressed. "Then what's wrong?"

She looked up at him with an expression he'd never seen before. Somewhere between shock and hardness, disbelief and pleasure. It was an odd expression.

"My dad said that he was listening to the news radio out in his truck," she said. "One of the headlines was a cop killer getting killed by a rival gang."

"Okay... so?"

"It was the same guy who ordered the hit on my family."

Reed made a good show at being surprised. "Seriously?"

She nodded. Then, her eyes filled with a lake of tears and she slapped both hands over her mouth. "Yes," she wept. "Oh, my God, Reed, he's dead. He was killed along with his brothers yesterday. He's really dead!"

She began to sob deeply and Reed went to her, putting both arms around her and holding her tightly. "Hey, now," he whispered. "It's okay. Don't cry. The guy lived by the sword and he died by the sword. That's not surprising."

She continued to weep. "I know," she said. "But... I don't even know how to process this. Is this really happening?"

Reed lifted his big shoulders. "If your dad said he heard it on the radio, then it must have."

Kinley wept for a few moments longer, overcome. "I

feel... I feel like it's like the end of a nightmare," she said. "I never thought I'd see this day, but here it is. The guy who caused me such pain is gone and I just can't believe it."

He gave her a squeeze, trying to give her some comfort. "It's shocking, for sure," he said. "And very coincidental that you would be in California when the guy was killed. Like karma."

She sniffled. "So weird," she agreed. "But... my God, I'm just stunned."

Reed didn't say anything more, fearful he might somehow incriminate himself. He was watching her reaction very carefully, however, concerned he might have put more of a burden on her somehow than actually bringing her relief. He'd hoped that it would bring her comfort, but maybe the comfort would be down the line somewhere after the shock had passed.

But he didn't regret what he did.

Not for one damn moment.

"Are you okay?" he asked gently. "Do you want to go back outside to your mom and dad? Maybe this is something you should be working through with them. They went through it, too, you know. They went through it without you."

She looked up at him. "You know what?" she said, wiping her face. "You're right. You're absolutely right. Would you mind if I went outside with them for a few minutes?"

He let her go. "Of course not," he said. "Go. I'll wander out in a minute."

She stood on her tip toes and kissed him. "Thank you," she said, kissing him again. "Thank you so much. For being here. For everything. Just... thank you."

"You sure you're okay?"

Kinley had to think about that. He could almost see the emotions rolling through her mind, but after a moment, she nodded.

She nodded like she meant it.

"Yes," she said. "I really think I am. Or, at least, I'm going to be."

He smiled at her, letting her kiss him one more time before she scooted out, heading to the parking lot where her parents were just greeting Tom's parents as they got out of their car. It was Bob who delivered the news about the dead gang member to Tom's parents and after that, the five of them processed the news together. Shock turned to disbelief, and disbelief for hope.

Hope turned to healing.

This was the turning point.

And that was what Reed had hoped for. He'd righted a wrong and felt no guilt. No remorse. He'd do it again a thousand times over if he had to, anything to give Kinley the peace she deserved. A religious man might have turned to God and forgiveness towards those responsible for the death of Kinley's family, but not Reed.

He wasn't in the business of forgiveness.

There were two reasons for that stance right in front of him. Children who had their lives unfairly cut short. As Reed stood in the quiet mausoleum, he looked over at

Violet and Liam's crypt again, his gaze lingering on three little words.

Sleep well, Angels.

Reaching out, he put his fingers on the marble.

"Everything is okay now," he whispered. "Your mom's going to be okay, I promise. I got her. And I got you, too."

He wait a few more moments before beginning his path out of the mausoleum, moving slowly across the marble, thinking on what lay ahead now for him and Kinley. An eventual return to Riverton and then...? He wasn't sure after that, but one thing he did know was that he was never going to be without her. He was going to marry her if he had to beg, plead, and cry for her agreement. To call Kinley his wife seemed like the only thing he'd ever wanted in his entire life. That beautiful, resilient, determined woman who had stepped on him, left him, left him again, before finally realizing she didn't have to run anymore. No one was running anymore unless it was to each other.

And he'd be waiting for her with open arms.

Reed was at the other end of the long line of crypts, heading for the door, when he thought he heard something behind him. A high-pitched sound, like a bird. Or even a giggle. Pausing, he turned around to see that there was no one behind him. No one else in the mausoleum. But looking up to the enormous stained glass rosette window on the wall, he could see that the window didn't look like a rosette at all. It looked like a sun. A big, bright yellow rising sun.

Much like a little girl would have drawn for him.

When he realized that, he chuckled to himself. Clearly, he was hearing things and seeing signs, but he didn't much care. He'd done what he'd come to California to do. He righted a wrong and he could live with it. There were times in days past when men would kill or die for a woman, and for Reed McCoy, those days of chivalry weren't gone. If he had it to do all over again, he would.

With a smile on his lips, he winked in the general direction of Violet and Liam's crypt.

Everything was going to be okay, indeed.

EPILOGUE
A YEAR LATER, RIVERTON, WYOMING, THE COFFEE CAKERY

IT WAS STANDING ROOM ONLY.

On-duty and in a hurry, Reed entered the fragrant restaurant. There were people waiting for tables as well as waiting for counter space because the lunch counter was full. The kitchen was running at full steam and the wait staff were running around, quickly and efficiently.

And then, he spied her.

"Dammit," Reed hissed to no one in particular. "What's she doing at the counter again?"

It really wasn't a question, but more a frustrated statement from a husband who couldn't seem to keep his pregnant wife off her feet. At thirty-seven weeks pregnant with a big baby boy, that she take it easy, but those words didn't exist in her Kinley's doctor had suggested vocabulary. In fact, the doctor wanted her to stay home and off her feet until the baby was born, but that kind of thing wasn't in Kinley's wheelhouse. She knew she wasn't supposed to be working much less filling in for a server at the lunch counter and when she saw Reed, she sighed unhappily and put both hands up.

He walked right up to the counter and scowled at her.

"*What* are you doing?" he demanded gently.

Kinley knew she was caught. "Look," she said, arms still up. "I'm surrendering. I'll go peacefully."

"No, you won't."

"No, I won't."

The man at the end of the counter got up and Reed took his seat, still-warm, and removed his regulation cowboy hat and put it on the countertop. With a contrite expression, Kinley gave him a glass of ice water and told the manager to have a BLT with fruit made for him. Then, she simply leaned on the counter and tried to look properly submissive as he frowned.

"I knew you'd be here," he said. "When I called your cell and then the house, and you didn't pick up either, I knew you'd be here."

She was trying to defend an indefensible position. "One of the servers called in sick," she said. "Look how busy we are – I couldn't just sit on my ass while the restaurant struggled."

He snorted. "Look at this place," he said, gesturing to the busy restaurant behind him to prove his point. "Kinley, I have news for you. It's not suffering."

She hung her head. "I'll go home after the lunch crowd, I promise."

He picked up his ice water and drained it. "Nope," he

said, setting the glass down. "You'll go home when I finish my sandwich. That's all the time you get, so if you have anything to wind up, do it now."

Knowing she had no choice, she went over to the manager and told the man she was being forced to go home when Reed was finished with his lunch. The manager, a young man with a degree in hospitality, just grinned and called out to Reed over Kinley's head.

"I told her not to come," he said. "I told her you'd come for her."

Reed nodded, an angry sort of nod, and pointed an accusing finger at Kinley, who took the hint when she realized not even her manager was on her side. She stuck her tongue out at him and picked up Reed's sandwich order just as it appeared in the window. Putting it in front of her husband, she refilled his water glass.

"What time are we going to the airport?" she asked, trying to change the subject.

He had a mouthful of sandwich. "I want to leave about six," he said. "Are you sure you want to go? It's a long drive to the airport, honey. You can just as easily wait for your parents at home."

Kinley shook her head. "I want to go," she said. "When are Christopher and Jackson getting in again?"

"Friday," he told her. "I feel like I haven't seen them in forever."

"Since Christmas does seem like forever."

"Are you sure you can put them to work here?"

She looked around. "Of course," she said. "They're a

little young, so I can't really have them do any heavy labor, but they can sweep floors and throw out trash. I'll pay them with pie. Hey, that reminds me - do you want a piece of pie?"

"What kind?"

"Boysenberry."

"Load me up."

With a grin, she went to get him a piece of pie and ice cream as he wolfed down the rest of his sandwich. He was nearly done when his parents came into the restaurant, heading to the counter when they caught sight of him and Kinley. Harmon and Shirley were regular fixtures at The Coffee Cakery and made it a point to come at lunchtime because they knew their son would be there, but they also came in to find out how Kinley and the baby were doing, like there was no other baby in the entire world soon to be born.

Truthfully, Kinley loved how in love with the new baby they already were.

A table opened up and they went to sit, but Reed was slower to move. He still had pie, and now a half a cup of coffee his wife had thoughtfully poured him, and he was savoring every bite. But that didn't mean that the clock wasn't ticking on Kinley.

"I'm almost done here," he said, realizing she was giving him more food and coffee in an effort to delay her departure. "Go get your purse. I'm taking you home myself."

Kinley shook her head. "My car is still here," she said. "I'll drive home."

"I'm going to follow you the whole way."

It was her turn to scowl. "You are a terribly suspicious person, you know that?"

"By nature," he said. "I'm trained to be suspicious. In your case, I have good reason."

She made a face at him, but resistance was futile. "Fine," she said. "I'll go get my purse."

He watched her go. From the back, she didn't look pregnant at all. She still had her delicious curves. It was only when she turned around that she looked like she had stuffed a very big pumpkin into her shirt. Reed had relished every single day of that pregnancy, even when she hadn't, because he was so in love with the woman who was bearing his child. It was a dream he never thought he'd achieve, he'd told her. Sometimes at night, he'd lay with his head against her belly, talking to his son, telling him how excited he was to meet him.

But he wasn't ready to meet him until the baby was full term.

Even if the mother didn't want to cooperate.

As Reed waited for her to return, he finished up his pie and drained the coffee cup, thinking that he needed to lay off the pie because his belts were starting to get tight. He was just about to go over to his parents' table to wait out Kinley when a young server from the back of the restaurant approached him.

"Reed?" the young woman said. "Kinley wants you."

"Where is she?"

"In her office."

Picking up his hat, he headed back to the rear of the restaurant where Kinley's office was, only to find her standing next to her desk in a somewhat strange position. She was leaning on the desk with her feet apart.

"What are you doing?" he asked.

She looked at him with a tight-lipped expression. "If you say I told you so, I'm going to kill you," she said.

"Told you so about what?"

"My water just broke."

His eyes widened. "Oh, Christ," he muttered, all humor out of his expression as he went to her to see a small puddle staining the carpet at her feet. "Are you in any pain?"

"My back hurts," she said. "But it's kind of been doing that for a week, so I didn't think anything of it."

Reed put his hands on her arms in a firm, comforting gesture. "Don't move," he said. "Understand? I want you to stay right here. I'm going to go tell my parents and ask them to pick up your parents at the airport and then I'm going to bring the unit around to the back door."

She grunted. "You'd better hurry up."

He took that to mean things were going on that she wasn't telling him about, so he kissed her swiftly and bolted out of the office. He told his parents, who were understandably excited, and the manager, who looked a little startled, before rushing out to his cruiser and pulling it around back. By the time he got there, Kinley was standing in the back door.

"I'm not kidding when I say you need to hurry," she said as he helped her into the car. "Light up those rotators and fly, McCoy, or you might be delivering this baby in the front seat of your cruiser."

He helped her put the seatbelt on. "If I didn't love you so much, I would seriously kill you right now," he said, kissing her quickly. "I'll be mad later."

She nodded, wincing as she rubbed her big belly. "*Much* later."

The truth was that Reed never kept that vow. One hour and twelve minutes later, Kinley delivered a nine-pound baby boy at Mountain View Regional Hospital and Reed forgot all about his frustration with her. The moment he held Wyatt Harmon McCoy in his arms, he forgot about everything.

But he also remembered a few things, too.

As Kinley slept after the fast, hard delivery, Reed held his new son into the night, telling him about his parents, how they met, and all about his siblings, two of whom were coming to visit in a few days. He also told him about Violet the artist and Liam the zookeeper, and about Violet's drawings that Grandparents Bob and Linda had framed and sent to Wyoming to hang on the nursery wall so Wyatt would be surrounded by reminders of the siblings he would never meet. There were also stuffed lions and gorillas in his room that had belonged to Liam. Little pieces of memories that would blend in with Wyatt's memories and become part of his childhood.

Into the night, Reed told Wyatt all of these things.

And Kinley had heard most of it.

Lying in bed, facing away from Reed and the baby, she had listened to Reed tell the baby a story she'd once told him about Violet and Liam and how they'd gotten lost at the Los Angeles Zoo once and after twenty minutes of panic, were found at the gorilla habitat, sitting on one side of the plexiglass while a big male silverback sat on the other, keeping an eye on them until their parents found them.

At least, that's what Liam had told them.

Reed wondered aloud if Wyatt would have gorilla adventures, too.

With a smile on her lips and tears in her eyes, Kinley drifted back to sleep listening to Reed's soft voice. It was bliss, joy, and heavenly all rolled into one. Four years ago when she came to Riverton, she could have never imagined how her life would turn out. A new husband, a new family, and a future that only held joy and love.

Perhaps running away from her past hadn't been the best thing she'd ever done, but it had been an important thing. A pivotal thing. She'd run straight into the arms of an angel who had literally saved her life. A destroyer angel who had gone above and beyond for her in ways Kinley would never know, but in ways that balanced out the universe in which they lived.

A destroyer angel who had been rewarded in his own right.

And a broken woman who was broken no more.

ABOUT THE AUTHOR

KATHRYN LE VEQUE is a critically acclaimed, USA TODAY Bestselling author (having hit the list over 30 times), an Indie Reader bestseller, a charter Amazon All-Star author, and a #1 bestselling, award-winning, multi-published author in Medieval Historical Romance with over 150 published novels. Kathryn also writes Romantic Suspense as Kat Le Veque.

Kathryn has received praise for her writing and has won several awards for her work, including two nominations for the Holt Medallion. Her books have topped best-seller lists, and she has gained a loyal fan base that eagerly anticipates each new release.

Kathryn is a talented author who has made a significant impact on the world of historical romance fiction. Through her captivating storytelling and meticulous research, she has enchanted readers with her tales of love, adventure, and the enduring power of the human spirit.

Kathryn loves to hear from her readers. Please find Kathryn on Facebook at Kathryn Le Veque, Author, or join her on Twitter @kathrynleveque, and don't forget to visit her website at www.kathrynleveque.com.

ALSO BY KAT LE VEQUE

The Unholy Angels

Hour of Surrender

Hour of Secrets

Hour of Dreams

Trent Chronicles

Valley of Shadow

The Eden Factor

Canyon of the Sphinx

The Eagle Brotherhood

The Sunset Hour

The Killing Hour

The Secret Hour

The Unholy Hour

The Burning Hour

The Ancient Hour

The Devils Hour

www.ingramcontent.com/pod-product-compliance
Lightning Source LLC
Chambersburg PA
CBHW050311110726
47899CB00007B/2203